"Well, Kyle, where's the new experience you promised?"

He hesitated slightly. "It's me, Julie. All of me."

"But, Kyle . . . ," I protested weakly as he gathered me into his arms.

"Remember, it's just like ice cream."

I was scared, but at the same time it was appealing. I knew we cared so much for each other. And I *did* love ice cream.

Kyle began to kiss me softly on my ear and neck, and I began to melt. *Once won't hurt,* I told myself. *What's the purpose in waiting anyway? Besides, no one gets pregnant the first time. . . .*

Just Like Ice Cream

Lissa Halls Johnson

Tyndale House Publishers, Inc.
Wheaton, Illinois

© 1982, 1995 by Lissa Halls Johnson
All rights reserved
Living Books is a registered trademark of Tyndale House Publishers,
Inc.

Published in association with the literary agency of Alive Communications, P.O. Box 49068, Colorado Springs, CO 80949.

Library of Congress Catalog Card Number 95-60236
ISBN 0-8423-1989-1

Printed in the United States of America

01 00 99 98 97 96
7   6   5   4   3

For Lee Roddy

Who taught me, loved me,
believed in me, prayed for me—

and who regularly hit me upside my
*   frizzy little head with a 2x4.*

Thanks, Uncle George!

_1_

THE radio crackled and fizzed. I leaned over the stack of unfolded clothes, adjusting the tuner.

The vibrant, sure voice of the DJ throbbed in my small room. "KBAY wings you back to the peak of the heat to bring you this former number one hit tune. So put on your summer gear and dream of the lazy days gone by."

> You are my fantasy,
> My life, my love.
> I'll never leave you
> For another, another.
> I'll never leave you, my love.

I couldn't believe it. I never thought I'd hear this song again. . . . Suddenly I forgot about the pile of laundry that Mom had asked me to fold.

I stood there, biting my bent finger to prevent uncon-trollable sobs as the tears started to run in torrents down my face. The song spoke of love and hope. To me it spoke of lies, of hurt. Of irreversible pain and loss.

> You are the one forever and today.
> You are the one for always.
> I'll never leave you,
> I love you and I care.
> I'll never leave you,
> I'll always be there.

"Oh, Kyle, you liar!"
I wanted to scream, but the sound stuck in my throat. Instead, I let the song sweep me back to the time before Kyle. The time before the pain.
Too much had been lost. Innocence, love. Even a life. So much that I could never gain back.
I know lots of girls would do it over again if they had the chance. But me? No.
No way.

• • •

The heat warmed our backs to an almost unbear-able temperature. I turned to walk backwards as I spoke to Stephanie. "I wonder if Carol had her baby yet?" I caught a drip from my ice-cream cone at the last second.

Stephanie looked at me crossly. "What do you care?"

"I dunno. Just curious, I guess."

"Guess I'm curious, too." Stephanie tossed her head, shaking her golden hair away from her sticky cone. "I do feel kind of sorry for her."

"So why don't *you* talk to her?" I urged. Stephanie had constantly tried to get me to talk to Carol at school. We had an ongoing argument about the whole thing.

"I said I feel sorry for her," Stephanie snapped back. "I didn't say I wanted to be buddies or anything." Then she looked thoughtful again. "She's nuts to keep her baby. No more fun, no more dates. Just baby all the time."

"Oh, come on, Steph, babies are adorable," I teased. "You can take them with you everywhere."

Stephanie's eyebrows raised. "Even on a date?"

"You've got a point," I replied reluctantly.

"You'll never find me with a puffer belly like that," Stephanie said, using her favorite term for pregnant.

"Me neither," I agreed.

Stephanie looked at her watch and said hastily, "Gotta run, Julie. I'm going to be late for work."

As she ran to her bike, I waved. Turning to walk down the hill to the park, I thought about our friendship. I'd never had such a close friend before. Through fights and fun we'd always stuck together. We understood each other so well, we didn't need explanations about our behavior. I doubted there was anything so awful that it could separate us. My dad always shook his head over our inseparability. "The gruesome two-some," he called us.

Comparing myself to Steph wasn't difficult. She had everything I lacked. She was gorgeous. If her blonde hair and perfect body weren't enough to catch the attention of every male in a one-block radius, her personality would. Even now, if I looked back to watch her pedaling to work, I would see cars slowing down as they passed and male heads turning to look.

I suppose I'm not too bad looking. People tell me all the time that I'm cute. But it's hard to believe them. I'd always thought Stephanie's blonde curly hair was far prettier than my sol-emn, straight brown strands. And I didn't think my body had caught up with my age. Maybe it never would.

Sighing deeply, I sat down in the grass. I thought at sixteen your body was supposed to have fancy curves to it. Nothing fancy about my curves.

The warm sun shifted my thoughts to a better world, one where I could be whoever I wanted and look as great as I wanted. I kicked back and closed my eyes.

A low whistle soon pierced my daydream. Slowly opening my eyes, I looked up to see crys-tal blue eyes and a grin wide enough to be on any toothpaste commercial. Embarrassed, I reverted to my feel-at-ease tactic. Teasing. "Haven't I seen you on TV?"

"Not yet, sweet babe," he teased back.

"Why do you call me *sweet* babe?" I asked. "You can't know if the treat is sweet until you taste it." I was shocked at my boldness. That simply wasn't like me.

The grin actually grew wider. "OK, *possibly* sweet babe, how about a taste? Meet you here Wednesday at six."

Now surprised by his boldness, but overwhelmed by the total *him,* I accepted.

I shielded my eyes to watch him pedal away when I realized we hadn't even exchanged names. I had to look away quickly when the sun reflected from a car bumper next to him, temporarily blinding me like a camera flash. Forcing myself up off the grass, I walked home in a daze. Sighing, I could still see that tanned body, with muscles in all the right places.

I chuckled to myself, wondering how I could have possibly noticed those flawless proportions after his sparkling blue eyes had held mine so steadily.

I jumped the two stairs to our porch and popped inside the house. "Hi, Mom," I said cheerfully. She winced as the door slammed.

"Must you—"

"Mom, can I go out night after tomorrow?"

She looked up from the sink. "Don't you baby-sit for Jan?"

"No, that's Friday night." She made a move to

slap my hand when I stole a carrot she had just peeled.

Tucking a wisp of hair behind her ear, she said absently, "I suppose it's OK. . . . Now get busy and set the table."

As I unstacked the dishes, I thought how lucky it was that she hadn't asked who I was going out with. She would think it pretty tacky for her precious little girl to go on a date with a nameless somebody.

Tuesday. I thought about him all day. Not romantically, though. I just let my mind ponder the possibilities of who he could be and where he came from.

That evening I went to Jan's, and her little eighteen-month-old boy, Stevie, took my mind off him at least for a while.

I never tire of baby-sitting for Stevie. Maybe it's because I enjoy his mother and father so much. Jan and Rick are probably the neatest people I have ever met. They make me feel so comfortable. I can be myself around them and not be afraid they will look at me weird if I say or do anything off-the-wall.

I love the way they tease each other with love shining in their eyes. It all sounds so gushy to tell it, but they really do love each other a lot. Their only fault is sometimes they talk about God. I usually just ignore it.

Jan had been a very special friend for a year and a half now, so I knew I could tell her all about my date. She laughed when I told her I didn't even know the name of the guy I would be going out with.

Wednesday morning I let myself float into wakefulness. What a yummy feeling. I looked at the clock. Nine. Counting the hours until six, I decided what I needed to accomplish before then. Sitting up suddenly, I cried out in horror. "Oh no! What if he doesn't show up? Maybe he talked to me just to take up air space. To be nice."

"Jule, are you talking to me?" my mom called.

"No, Mom." I plunked back down on my stomach. Now what should I do? As I stepped into the shower, I decided to go, just in case.

Walking to the park at five-forty-five, I kept checking my reflection in the store windows. I pretended to be browsing, though—I wouldn't want anyone to think I'm stuck on myself. I noticed that my new white lace top, barely meeting my jeans, showed off my tan nicely. I could hardly wait to see his look.

If he was there.

As I walked down the final hill to the park, a sharp *slap, slap, slap* occupied my attention. The noise of my flip-flops was bouncing off the building walls and echoing back at me.

Then I heard that mellow voice drifting up to me. "Hey, possibly sweet babe. I hope those flip-flops are bringing you in this direction."

I looked down the hill to see a very handsome figure lying under a tree. "Well, they *are* on a voice command," I yelled in return. "I pro-grammed them to your voice."

"Is that all I am to you?" The grin was back. "Just a voice?"

Approaching him, I stuck my hands in the back pockets of my jeans, returning the smile. "That's all you are until I get a name out of you."

"If a name will help, it's Kyle. Kyle Browning. And what, may I ask, is yours, possibly sweet babe?"

Putting my hands on my hips, I tilted my head to one side. "I don't know if I should tell you."

He laid back, hands behind his head, and closed his eyes. "Makes no difference to me," he said calmly. "I'll just make up my own name for you."

"And what might that be?"

"Oh . . ." He looked at me through one squinting eye. "Something that suits you . . ." He closed his eye. "Bozo, maybe."

I kicked his foot. "Julie suits me better than Bozo."

The eye opened again, this time coupled with a raised eyebrow. "Oh, I don't know about that." The grin came back in full force as he sat back up, crossing his legs. He began to pull and toss individual blades of grass. "Julie what?"

I plopped down beside him. "Not Julie What. Julie Marshall."

"Hello, Julie Marshall," he said, sticking out

his right hand. "Glad to meet you. Was that proper enough?"

I answered with an ugly look.

He suddenly jumped up, grabbing my hand in the process and pulling me up, too. He let go as soon as I stood. As I brushed off the seat of my jeans, he said, "How does a sandwich sound?"

"I don't know." I smirked. "I've never listened to one."

Shaking his head, Kyle asked, "Sweet babe, are you hungry for a sandwich?"

I tossed my head back and laughed. "Sure."

On the way to the deli we talked about all the usual stuff. About my dad being in construction, his in real estate. About my older brother, Matt, and younger sister, Tammy. His lack of any. About the fact that he lived in my town during the summer and in San Francisco, or "the city" as we called it, during the school year.

My heart dropped a couple notches when I heard that. Obviously he was in no place to commit himself to a long-term friendship with me. I filed the information away and continued the discussion, which had now progressed to family pets.

It seemed as though the only things we accomplished during dinner were filling our stomachs and laughing a lot. We finally decided it was time to remove ourselves from the deli before someone else did it for us.

The rest of the evening we spent walking all over town. I could say we talked, but that would almost be a lie since we spent most of the time laughing.

I did learn he loved music, and he discovered my favorite love is ice cream.

Although we didn't talk much, I felt I really knew him when he walked me to my door. He surprised but pleased me when he didn't try to kiss me good-night. I'm shy about kissing on the first time out. Then the thought slid through my brain, *Maybe he didn't really enjoy himself.*

"See you tomorrow," he said quietly.

"Bye," I answered as he loped off the porch and lifted his hand in response. I wondered if I really would see him again.

"Oh, I hope so," I said softly in the darkness. "I really hope so."

2

THURSDAY morning. Pure pittsville. I waited until Mom left for work before dragging my body out of bed. I didn't want all the usual light talk about how my date went. I knew I would only be able to answer, "It went all right . . . right out the door."

After my shower, I poured some Cheerios into a plastic mug and sat down to watch the morning game shows. I thought about calling Stephanie as I had promised, but I didn't know what to tell her either.

As I munched the Cheerios, all I could think about was Kyle and what I might have done to make him never want to see me again.

The phone rang for the fourth time. "Hello," I said hesitantly.

"What's the deal?" a familiar voice said jokingly.

My voice shook a little. "What do you mean?"

"I'm down here at the park, and the one I'm here to see is either invisible or not present."

"And who might that person be?" I asked dumbly.

"You, my little nut."

I couldn't speak. I knew if I did, I would say something stupid. He had been out *looking* for me!

"Well? . . ."

"Well, what?" I stammered.

"Well, are you coming to the park or not?"

"Give me an hour." I hoped he wouldn't change his mind.

Kyle became so silent I knew he must have decided against seeing me. "An *hour?* . . . OK. Instead, meet me at that ice-cream place on the corner."

Relief filled my voice. "Kramer's? OK."

I hung up the phone with one finger, then pushed autodial for Steph. I told her all about Kyle while choosing my best kick-around clothes and dressing in record time. Flying out the front door, all I could think of was the joy of seeing Kyle again. He had kept his word. I was going to see him today!

I tried walking slowly to Kramer's, a futile attempt to hide my excitement. Kyle pushed the door open from the inside. "What took you so long?" he asked impatiently.

I looked at my watch. "Only one hour and five minutes. . . . What's your rush?"

Kyle hesitated and seemed uneasy for the first time since I had met him. "I just hoped to see you before I left for the city today."

My heart dropped. He was going back.

"It's only for one night. I'll be back tomorrow. Can we go to a movie?"

"Not unless it's on TV. I have to baby-sit."

"Can't you cancel?" Kyle sounded as though he might be pleading.

"Sorry. It's for Jan." My voice made it sound like I needed to go to a funeral. "She depends on me. I promised last week." For once I wished I wasn't so loyal.

"Who is Jan?" Kyle demanded.

"She's a friend." I waited until the waitress served our sandwiches before continuing. "Why don't you come over there? They leave at six. Stevie goes to bed at seven. So if you come at seven-thirty—"

"I'll be there," Kyle broke in eagerly.

Drawing him a map on my napkin, he looked at it and nodded. He stuffed it into his pocket, then looked at me and flashed his grin. Popping the last bite of sandwich into his mouth, he said quickly, "See you, Julie. Tomorrow at seven-thirty." As he stood up, he leaned over and kissed me on the cheek.

I never even saw him ride away on his bike—
or Stephanie arrive on hers.

Chewing my sandwich slowly, I looked up to
see her rushing to my table smiling from ear to
ear. "Who's the *hunk?*" she asked.

Smiling coyly, I answered, "Kyle."

Disbelief registered on her face. *"That* is Kyle?"

"Sure is," I said, trying to act indifferent.

We continued discussing Kyle through our
sandwiches, ice cream, shopping . . . all the way
until Stephanie had to go to work.

At home, it was easy to tell Mom what Kyle
and I had done the night before, now that I
knew he might be around for a little while.

Friday dragged on until I thought I couldn't
wait another minute to see Kyle.

I didn't tell Jan that Kyle would be coming
over. That was a first. I always tell Jan everything.
But I couldn't risk her saying no. I wanted so
badly to see him that night.

After I put Stevie to bed, I checked the clock
every two minutes. I sat in one chair, then
another. I picked up every magazine, bouncing
my foot as I flipped through the pages without
really seeing them. I must have looked at myself
in the mirror twenty times before the doorbell
finally rang.

"Come in," I said formally. Kyle didn't look
nervous at all. "Have a good trip?"

"Of course not," he said with a smile.

Sitting on the edge of the couch I asked, "Why not?"

He slipped his arm around me as he sat down. "Because I missed you."

"I missed you, too," I said quietly. Afraid to look at his face, I looked at his foot where it rested on his knee.

Kyle gently took hold of my chin and turned my face to his. "Did you really?"

I nodded my head.

His kiss was soft and gentle. So unlike anyone else I had ever kissed before. I thought I would melt right into the couch.

Backing away, Kyle looked right into my eyes. "I knew it!"

"What?" I asked, afraid he didn't like my kiss.

Kyle kissed me again and said, "You *are* a sweet babe. I'm a good judge of things like that."

I just smiled, and he kissed me again.

"Julie, while I was gone I heard a new song I thought you might enjoy, so I bought you the tape." He slipped a small package from his hip pocket.

"Thanks!" I said eagerly. Taking the tape, I tore off the cellophane and headed for Jan's stereo. "Which song is it?" I called over my shoulder.

"'I'll Never Leave You.' First song, second side." I popped the tape in and turned it on.

You are my fantasy,
My life, my love.

I clasped my hands together and turned to look at Kyle. My eyes questioned the meaning of the words.

I'll never leave you
For another, another.
I'll never leave you, my love.

The song continued, and Kyle's smile drew me across the room. I cuddled up to him and put my head on his shoulder.

You are the one forever and today.
You are the one for always.
I'll never leave you,
I love you and I care.
I'll never leave you,
I'll always be there.

When the sweet melody finished, I turned to Kyle and kissed him. "Thanks," I said softly, looking right into his eyes.

"I guess that was worth spending my money on."

"You—!" I said, slapping him gently on his arm.

The rest of the evening we cuddled and watched an old John Wayne rerun. During the commercials, we either talked or kissed. (I liked the kissing best.)

I hated for the night to end. I had never felt so

loved and cared for in my life. My parents didn't often show much love or affection to me—or to each other, for that matter. Besides, even if they had, this was different. Someone thought I was special. Someone who didn't have to think so.

When we parted, I reluctantly let go of his hand with the promise that we would meet at the park in the morning.

Days began to fly by. Every day overflowed with thoughts of Kyle or with time spent with him. I had no time for anything else. Every moment began and ended with Kyle.

We rode bikes and horses. We went waterskiing with friends. We hiked and picnicked and played.

Over and over I listened to the tape he had given me, always taking special notice of "our" song.

Stephanie began to fade out of my life. The only time I would see her would be when Kyle and I were getting ice cream at Kramer's. She always had a new guy in tow and seemed more distant each time. I didn't really care. If she didn't understand that we could still be friends . . .

It felt like more than three weeks since Kyle and I had first met in the park when the sweltering day arrived that began to change my whole life.

On that day, my craving for an ice-cream cone consumed me more than usual. Lying on my bed, I longed for one desperately. I counted my change and didn't even have enough for a single scoop.

When the phone rang, I halfheartedly reached over and said weakly, "Hello."

"Hi, sweet babe, how about a double scoop today?"

"Ummm. Sounds perfect."

"Meet me at Kramer's?"

"You bet!"

"OK, I'll give ya ten."

I ran the brush through my hair, but something kept bugging me. I frowned, thinking, and realized something in Kyle's voice had sounded different. Smoother than usual, maybe. I tried to ignore it, figuring my imagination was running away with me again.

"See ya, Mom," I yelled as I skipped the bottom three steps. "Ice cream with Kyle."

"Bye, Jule. Glad to see you've got him so well trained."

"Oh, *Mother.*"

I could hear my mother yelling after me as I ran out the door. "If you aren't careful you'll get fat from too many ice-cream cones."

I just shook my head.

Kyle must have called from Kramer's, because when I got there he held a half-eaten cone in one hand and a whole but melting strawberry cone in the other. Strawberry! My favorite. He was licking around the edge of my strawberry cone.

"Hey, you. I think your tongue is attracted to the wrong cone," I said, pouting.

"How do you know it's yours, sweet babe?"

"Why, it's got my name right on it." I grabbed the cone before he could eat any more of that precious stuff. We walked away from the shop, finally getting some relief from the heat as the ice cream seemed to fill our veins.

Kyle watched me eat my cone, and he smiled. "You love ice cream, don't you, Julie?"

"It's the best," I agreed.

"What if you never had any ice cream until you were twenty-five. Say your parents protected you and felt it wasn't good for you. Say you finally had some and found out you loved it like you do now. Wouldn't you be disappointed that you hadn't started enjoying it sooner in life?"

"Why, of course, Kyle," I answered, a little confused.

"Well, my little sweet babe, I want you to try something just as good as ice cream. Something everyone regrets they didn't start enjoying sooner. Are you game?"

"Sure, Kyle, what is it?"

"Come with me and I'll show you."

A weird silence held us until we walked around the corner and he began to climb the steps to his house. I held back, feeling strange.

"Coming?" His eyes were pleading as his eyebrows raised with the question.

"I don't get it, Kyle."

"Just come on," he said, grabbing my hand and taking me up with him. We laughed as I tried to guess what this new experience could be.

"If it's caviar, you can forget it. I don't care if it *is* a delicacy. I'm not eating any fish eggs."

"It's not caviar, nut."

"If it's beer, you're too late. I had my first and last experience when I was fourteen. It makes me sick."

Kyle just laughed.

"Hey, Kyle," I said as the door opened into a quiet house. "Where's your mom? She's always here."

"She and Dad went to the city for the week. He had business, she had a wedding shower to attend."

"Oh, who's getting married?"

"Not important." His answer was curt as he pushed the door closed with his foot. Now his hands and arms were full of me. He had never kissed me so passionately before.

I gently pushed him away. "OK, so where's my new experience?"

He hesitated slightly. "Well, sweet babe. It's me."

"What do you mean, *you?*" I asked teasingly, hoping he didn't mean what I thought he did.

He tilted his head to one side, gathered me back into his arms, and said, "All of me."

"But, Kyle . . . ," I protested weakly.

"Remember. It's just like ice cream." He waited quietly while I let the thoughts rush through my mind. I was scared, but at the same time it was appealing. I knew we cared so much for each other. And I *did* love ice cream, and I would certainly have regretted never trying it until I was older.

Kyle began to kiss me softly on my ear and neck, and I began to melt. *Once won't hurt,* I told myself. *What's the purpose in waiting, anyway? Besides, no one gets pregnant the first time.*

I allowed myself to return his kisses just as passionately as he gave them.

It didn't take long for us to get our clothes off and climb into bed. I was surprised my nakedness didn't embarrass me. Maybe because he enjoyed it so much.

But then . . . it hurt. No one told me it would hurt. I wanted to cry out, but instead bit my lip.

When he finished, he kissed me once on the cheek, rolled over, and went to sleep. I couldn't cry. I wasn't really sad. Just ashamed. Also amazed. *That's it?* I thought to myself. *That's what everyone is talking about as marvelous?*

I got up slowly so I wouldn't wake Kyle. I felt funny as I walked to get my clothes. Suddenly I had to run to the bathroom as warm fluid dripped down my leg. *No one tells you anything!* I thought angrily.

I cleaned up and put my clothes back on, then sat down on a chair, watching Kyle sleep. I didn't know what else to do.

I couldn't even think.

3

I checked my watch. One hour and twelve minutes had passed when Kyle finally woke up. "Hi, babe!" he said cheerfully. "Are you glad you tried your first ice-cream cone?"

Smiling weakly, I lied. "Yeah. It was wonderful."

"C'mere." He beckoned with his finger.

I walked stiffly and sat on the edge of the bed. Kyle reached up and put his hands on my cheeks, pulling me down to kiss me gently. *How could someone kiss so sweetly and be so insensitive?* I thought angrily.

Kyle interrupted my thoughts. "Why did you put your clothes on? You were beautiful without them."

Something tightened inside of me. "Oh? What about with them on?" my voice accused.

"No, you know what I mean." He propped himself on his elbow. "Is something wrong?"

"I'm sorry, Kyle. It's . . ." I looked at the clock so I could lie again. "Oh, it's later than I thought. I need to get home to help Mom." I reluctantly kissed him on the cheek and fled out the door.

I avoided all the main streets on the way home, I was so afraid I might meet someone I knew. I didn't want anyone to see me. All I wanted to do was to get home and into the shower. What would I say to my family? What would I do?

Quietly, I got to my room and shed my clothes. I didn't want Mom to wash them. I would have to offer to do all the laundry. Yuck. But I guessed *anything* was better than her finding out.

I hid until dinnertime. I was panicking, certain everyone would *know* just by looking at me. But they didn't. And for them, everything went on normally for a Saturday night.

All evening I wished I had agreed to sit for Jan. At her house I wouldn't have to paint on smiles and force acceptable conversation. Bedtime brought relief, at least from the presence of family. But sleep wouldn't come and deliver me from my rushing thoughts.

Each time I closed my eyes I could feel Kyle's body against mine. I could feel his motion. The motion that rubbed me raw inside and out.

"What's wrong with me?" I pleaded silently.

"Why didn't I enjoy it?" I must have missed something to feel so confused and unsatisfied.

The rest of the week I allowed Kyle to make love to me whenever he wanted. Each time I expected to experience the thrill of sex. You know, the thrill everyone always talks about. But each time disappointed me. My disappointment seemed to increase as my physical pain decreased.

I did enjoy the affection. Kyle kissed, touched, and held me like I was something wonderful. His tender words of love softened my heart. "Julie, I love you," he would repeat over and over.

But soon he would become anxious, like he couldn't wait another second for his pleasure, and *my* pleasure lapsed into past tense.

"Sex changes your relationship," I had heard my friends' happy voices say more than once. Well, ours changed all right. I got more sullen as Kyle demanded more and grew less fun.

He swept up every spare moment of my life into his pocket as though it was all his. Before our "ice cream," I gave those moments over willingly, glad that he would want them. But now he grabbed them almost without my permission.

One week. Two weeks. Another day, another request.

Kyle's eager voice greeted me as I answered the phone. "Hi, sweet babe, how about meeting me for another ice cream?"

I wanted to turn him down but couldn't. Instead, I replied in mock excitement, "Of course, Kyle, that would be great." Hanging up the phone, I thought what a great little actress I had become these past three weeks.

I found Mom and told her it was ice-cream time again.

"Another ice cream?" she teased. "And so early in the morning! Kyle will go broke supporting your habit."

"Yeah, right," I said sarcastically. If she only knew whose habit was really being supported.

"Jule, what's come over you lately?" Mom asked with concern. "Your usual cheerful self has been overcome by some irritable and withdrawn monster."

"Yeah, right," I repeated as I slammed the back door.

My feet hit the pavement hard as I walked to meet Kyle. I wanted to talk with someone about my situation. I couldn't talk with Stephanie. We saw each other so rarely I hardly knew what she looked like.

"Julie!"

The voice startled me. I spun around. "Jan. I haven't seen you in so long . . . ," I said nervously.

"I know," she said, smiling. "You've been so preoccupied with Kyle you haven't had a chance to come even for a little visit. Right?"

I nodded slightly, twirling a small clump of hair around my finger. "I'm sorry, Jan," I apologized.

"That's OK, Julie. Stevie misses you."

As she spoke, I looked at the ground, bending and straightening my knee.

"Maybe you can stay away from Kyle long enough to baby-sit for us next week."

My mind was so preoccupied, it took a moment for me to realize she had asked a question. "Of course," I answered, trying to sound eager.

"Julie, is something wrong?" Jan pierced me with concerned eyes.

"Not really." Thinking quickly, I knew I had to lie again. Talking with Jan was my answer, but I didn't want her to know about Kyle and me. "I just heard Carol had her baby. A girl."

Jan broke in, "Great!"

"She's living in the city now. There are better job opportunities there." I paused, trying to think of the right way to put my next sentence. "But something about her situation bothers me. Can we talk?"

"Sure. Now?"

"No, I'm meeting Kyle now."

"How about tomorrow at one? We can go to Kramer's for an ice cream . . . my treat."

"Sure," I said, forcing a smile and excitement into my voice. Funny how the thought of ice cream didn't please me as much as it used to. I didn't even like to think about ice cream anymore.

But I couldn't exactly tell Jan I didn't want ice cream. Glancing at the bank's digital clock, I read

10:07, then 100 degrees. I was pretty well guaranteed another scorcher would come tomorrow, which meant there was no excuse to avoid ice cream.

"Hi, Stevie!" I said the next day as Jan arrived, pushing his stroller.

"Hi, Dulie," Stevie said excitedly in his little baby voice. "Ice cweam, ice cweam."

"In a minute," Jan replied impatiently. She turned to me. "Kids are wonderful, but sometimes . . ." She sighed and shook her head. "It's been a hard day."

We bought our ice cream and sat in the booth farthest from the counter. "So what about Carol is bothering you?" Jan asked after the typical small talk.

I wiped my sweaty palms one at a time on the back of my cutoffs. "Her situation has made me think about sex." I breathed deeply, trying to push the next words out. They felt as though they sat heavy on my chest. "Do you enjoy sex?" My voice cracked.

Not acting too surprised, Jan answered, "Sure, Julie, I love it. Why?"

I tried to act casual, licking my cone before I answered. I shrugged my shoulders. "I guess I just wondered what all the fuss is about. Why do people always seem to have sex on their minds? TV, movies, magazines—everybody is always talking about sex. I'm just wondering if it's really worth all the attention it gets."

Jan laughed. "Yes and no." She paused to give a bite of ice cream to Stevie. "It depends on your relationship. If that is right, sex is very special and satisfying. If it's not, it's scary—filled with guilt and dissatisfaction."

"What do you mean, a 'right' relationship?" I leaned over and gave Stevie a bite from my cone.

"I mean a marriage based on love and trust and commitment. I know Rick loves me and won't leave me tomorrow. I don't have to engage in sex to keep him. He cares about what pleases me in our sexual relationship and carries it through."

"You can have all that trust, love, and commitment without marriage," I said with faked assurance. Then I paused. I didn't have any of that with Kyle. No real security. Deep inside I was afraid it would be sex or good-bye. "So how could it be wrong for someone to have sex just because they're not married?" I kept on.

Jan shared more of her cone with a wiggly Stevie. "Because God says it is wrong, and for good reasons. He knows us quite well. After all, he made us, and he made sex. So he ought to know what he is talking about."

"OK," I interrupted. "Give me some of the reasons."

Jan tilted her head, thinking. "God doesn't give us rules at random. They're designed to protect us, and for some very basic, practical reasons.

First of all, there is the very real possibility of getting AIDS."

"Not if you're careful."

Jan frowned and continued. "Second are the many other viruses or infections you can get. And believe me, these are more common than any of us like to think."

"You mean STDs?"

She nodded. "They're getting worse. I talked to a doctor friend recently who told me of new infections plaguing teenage girls who had begun to have sex. These infections can be serious enough to cause sterility—and that means no babies. Ever."

I raised my eyebrows in mock interest but didn't say anything.

Jan continued, "God also wants you to enjoy sex completely."

I broke in again. "But most people think God doesn't want anyone to enjoy sex."

Jan laughed. "On the contrary, he wants you to have a great time with sex. That's why he set up marriage as the perfect place to enjoy it. In marriage, commitment is the shelter over your head. It protects your emotions and proves love."

"But I've heard it's awful to marry a virgin," I protested. "No experience, and all that. How can I be a good lover if I don't practice first?"

Jan winced. "I've heard that, too. But it's not true. Being a virgin is something special, for girls and for guys. Then you come into marriage with only each other to learn from. You learn what pleases your husband, and you aren't distracted by what pleased someone else. You start fresh. There aren't painful memories to overcome or fight against."

I looked at my napkin and asked bravely, "Then why do guys push so hard to have sex? Why is it so important to them?"

"First of all, guys push hard because God made most males with an incredible sex drive. Once their hormones get caught up in pleasure, it isn't easy for guys to turn back. And if they haven't had any training in responsibility and respect, they don't consider that pushing for sex is not kind—or right. It's good for them, so it must be good for everyone. Our society has continually affirmed this idea. Just consider the movies and TV shows you see, they're all full of sex—and they usually show it as something wonderful, something you shouldn't miss just because you're not married."

She was right. Some of my favorite TV shows almost always had at least one love scene. And it always made me feel like I was missing out on something.

Jan went on. "Some teenage guys are so wrapped up in their hormones they forget that the pleasure they are getting is a result of another human being giving up a part of themselves. Sometimes, outside the loving commitment of marriage, guys think of sex as a fun game for themselves. Either of these kinds of sex will consist of the act without much thought to the girl's enjoyment of it. He enjoyed it, and that's all that matters. At least, at that point. Sex can be purely selfish." She shook her head. "Sex is so much more than that."

"I don't think I understand all this," I lied. I knew exactly what she meant. I was experiencing it.

"I didn't either until I got married," Jan assured me. "I came to understand that sex is giving. Giving enjoyment to the one you love. Making him or her feel good. There is nothing wrong with that. God made our bodies in such a way that sex would make us feel good. When Rick and I got married, I was so glad for the wisdom of God, even though it hadn't really made sense to me before."

"So you were a virgin when you got married?"

"Yes. Both Rick and I were."

I stared at her.

Jan grinned. "It wasn't easy, believe me! Rick and I survived only with God's help, a lot of prayer, and strict avoidance of backseats and thick shrubbery." She chuckled, then shook her head, looking into the distance, remembering. "It was so hard!" Jan turned and looked me in the eyes. "But it was worth waiting. I have many friends who didn't and were sorry. Wait for sex, Julie— you won't regret it."

"Thanks a lot, Jan."

"Anytime, Julie. See you next Friday then?"

"Sure." I patted Stevie on the cheek, then kissed him. "Bye!"

As I walked home, a car drove slowly by, windows rolled down in a vain attempt to dispel the heat within.

"You are my fantasy," the radio blared, "my life, my love. I'll never leave you. . . ."

I couldn't stop the tears. Jan was right. There was only one way to stop hurting myself. I knew I had to tell Kyle good-bye.

4

"KYLE, I can't go on like this." I buried my face into his smooth chest.

He stroked my hair and my bare back. "Like what, sweet babe?"

I traced circles on his chest. "I want to break off our relationship. . . ."

"But why?" He sounded like a hurt puppy.

"I can't pretend anymore." His chest quickly became wet with my tears. "I can't pretend I enjoy sex because I don't. I hate it."

Instead of the gentle understanding I expected, he grabbed my arms and pushed me away to where he could look into my face. "What do you mean you don't enjoy sex?" he questioned angrily. "What a stupid reason to destroy a good relationship."

I just looked at him through blurry eyes, trying hard not to break into sobs.

He continued, "Sex with me is great! How can you *not* like it?"

I suddenly understood. "Your reputation is at stake, isn't it?" I almost shouted as I dried my cheeks. "If we break up, you're worried I'll tell someone you're bad in bed." I got out of bed and stomped over to the chair. I turned my back on him and pulled on my clothes.

As I turned to leave, I saw Kyle's lips were tight and his eyes narrowed. He kept silent as he watched me go.

I don't remember walking home. I ignored my sister when I got there, going straight to the phone. My hands shook as I flipped the pages of the phone book. LEWIS, P. I felt awful that I had forgotten the number.

"Stephanie," I tried to sound cheerful, "want to go see a movie tonight?"

She paused for a long time. "What happened, Kyle go to the city?" she asked snidely.

"No. I just thought . . . well . . . we haven't seen each other in a long time. . . ."

Her voice softened. "I'm sorry, Julie. I've felt so left out of your world lately."

"I know, Steph. I've left a lot of people out."

She rescued me. "I'll see you at seven then?"

"OK."

I'm glad the movie was supposed to be sad. It gave me an excuse to cry through the whole thing. Afterward I struggled through an ice cream at Kramer's. I tried hard not to cry, yet occasionally another tear would slip out. I waited until Stephanie bent over her hot fudge before I wiped my face.

Then she caught me. "Come on, Julie, the movie wasn't *that* sad," she teased. She tilted her head to one side as the smile left her face. "What's bugging you?"

I looked at her and attempted to speak. "Oh, Steph . . ." Tears rushed down my face. I could only shake my head, grab my purse, and race out the door.

Looking over my shoulder I could see a confused Stephanie tripping over people and chairs in her attempt to follow me out the door.

"Julie, Julie!" her voice pleaded in the darkness.

I continued to run until I turned a corner, certain she couldn't see me anymore. Slowing to a walk, I let my sorrow and anger flow unheeded.

When I reached home, the tears had dried, but my anger still bubbled and boiled inside.

A small note, written on a torn off corner of a magazine had been tacked to our message board over the phone. "Call Kyle." I figured my sister, Tammy, must have taken the message. At twelve, she couldn't be burdened with details.

As I wondered whether I should return the call and spit out my anger, the phone rang. "Hello?"

"Julie, I'm sorry."

Icicles laced my voice. "Me, too, Kyle."

"No, Jule. I'm sorry I made you so angry. You know I love you."

The icicles melted just a little. "I know, Kyle."

"Forgive me?"

"I guess so." Then the icicles were gone, and I blurted, "I love you, too."

"Then don't say good-bye."

He's right. I can't let him go, I thought.

Kyle the cunning. Kyle the fox. Kyle the masterpiece. He held my heart, gently, yet firmly.

"I won't," I whispered.

"And, Julie, I understand. We can lay off the sex for a week."

"Thanks," I replied. I knew he really didn't understand. He probably thought my emotions were jumbled because of my period. I frowned at the thought. What period? I never kept track because I was so irregular anyway. But I didn't tell Kyle that. I was too thankful for a week off from sex.

I enjoyed every minute of it. We chased kids off the swings, slides, and merry-go-round at the park so we could play. We called friends we hadn't seen in our previous weeks of being hermits, planning bike rides and swimming get-togethers.

Stephanie was often there, flirting with this guy or that one, always tossing her golden hair. Occasionally she threw me a concerned look, which I ignored. I still pretended the tears were over the movie.

And then the week was over.

Our first time back in bed showed me nothing had changed. My thrill never came. I always reached for the impossible goal. Whatever that was.

I tried to hide my discouragement. I even made excuses to get out of there and home to where I could rummage through all my feelings.

One night, when I closed the door to my room, I mechanically walked over and turned on the stereo. I slid the tape Kyle had given me into the player. Clamping on the earphones, I lay on the floor with my feet up on my bed.

"I'll never leave you . . ." drifted from ear to ear. The motion reminded me of something.

Seesaws! I hadn't been on a seesaw in years. I couldn't believe I'd ever liked them. They gave you a funny feeling in the pit of your stomach. Almost like you want to throw up, but not quite. My eyes widened. The same feeling happened every time I saw Kyle! Up, down. Up, down. Churning inside. Wanting to love him, not loving him. Wanting sex, not wanting sex.

But like any seesaw, it was hard to stop once it got started, and I didn't have strength enough to stop this one.

My seesaw was up, and my life was filled with joy when, to put it bluntly, we had our clothes on. When the clothes came off, the seesaw hit the ground with a jarring bump, jumbling my insides all over again.

"I AM NOT HAPPY," I would scream to no one and everyone. And no one heard my silent voice.

. . .

And so the seesaw days of August passed, each differing only slightly from the one before. The first few days of September pulled in the Labor Day weekend on a towrope.

Being the last official weekend of summer, Labor Day stirred up our town more than any other weekend of the whole year. Kyle and I made sure we were a part of every activity available. Then it, too, was over.

By Monday night most of the tourists had gone home, freeing the popular eating spots from the crowds. Kyle and I trooped into the deli for a sandwich.

"Here we are again," I reflected dramatically.

Kyle had suddenly grown quiet. "Yeah."

"C'mon, spoilsport. Let's be romantic and relive our first date." I crooned in total silliness.

It was as if Kyle hadn't heard me. "I'm leaving tomorrow, sweet babe."

I stopped short. "Oh, for how long?"

"Julie, where's your head? I'm going home. You know, back to the city . . . senior year . . . all that stuff."

I couldn't believe I had forgotten he would leave some day for the city. Permanently.

"Oh." I waited for the sadness to hit, but all I felt was relief. Why? I should be sobbing with grief.

He touched my hand. "I don't know when I'll see you again, little one."

"Not tomorrow?"

"No. We have to leave early."

"Won't you be able to come visit on weekends?"

Kyle twisted his napkin into uselessness. "Well, Julie . . . I'm not sure my parents will . . . uh . . . let me come alone."

"Come on, Kyle. They leave you here for weeks at a time alone, why can't they let you drive? You're a big boy now," I added sarcastically. "It's only three hours. . . ."

Kyle touched my lips with the tips of his fingers to quiet me. "You know the boss. There's no arguing with him."

That was true. But I couldn't believe his dad would not let him come see me. His dad called me his "little darlin'" and always lectured Kyle on "The Care and Feeding of Julie."

Here was the seesaw again. One second I frantically thought of ways for Kyle to visit, and the next, relief flooded me that I'd be free. Free from the pressure of frustrating lovemaking.

We walked to my house, hand in hand, taking

every long-cut possible. I looked at my watch. "Kyle, it's past my curfew. You can't come in."

"I know."

I turned to face him, taking his free hand in mine. "Kyle, I—"

I never finished my sentence. Kyle pulled my hands around his back, our fingers still laced together. He kissed the top of my head. Then as I looked up, we kissed once more.

Kyle touched the tip of my nose with his index finger. "I love you, Julie. Bye." He walked a few steps, turned and grinned. "Don't forget our song."

Just like that, he turned and left. Nothing fit together. Not my emotions, not his response. It didn't seem real that he would be leaving the next day. He had become a part of me. A day wouldn't seem right without him.

I knew love didn't end as easily as Kyle's good-bye. I turned to enter the house, confident Kyle would be back in a couple of weeks. He wouldn't last without me.

5

I'D blown it. All the time I'd known Jan, I'd listened with patience to her talk about Jesus. At least she didn't grab your collar, glare in your eye, and threaten you with hell if you didn't plead for mercy. You could tell Jesus was a big part of her life. She talked about him naturally. The same way I talked about Kyle.

Anyway, I felt really bad that I had laughed at her. I don't recall ever being so rude before.

It had happened the night before, when I was keeping Jan company while Rick was out of town. We were talking about family stuff when I began to share some of my feelings that were bothering me.

"You know, Jan, sometimes I think nobody loves me."

Jan was looking intently at the fabric on her sewing machine. "Why's that, Julie?"

"Oh, I don't know. Mom is so busy with work and all. She hardly has time to think of herself, much less me."

Jan nodded. "What about your dad?"

I shook my head, then began to twist my hair around my finger into a curl. "Dad is so quiet. Mom says his construction work wears him out. She says that he pours himself into his work so much that he doesn't have anything left for us when he gets home. Sometimes it seems the only time I hear his voice is when he's yelling at a referee or somebody on TV."

Jan looked up from her sewing. She said gently, "Julie, I think you know deep inside that they love you."

"Yeah, I guess so." I tapped my foot on the floor, avoiding her eyes. "I wish they would show it more often."

I looked up. Jan's head was bent over her machine again.

"Why can't we always be loved? I want Kyle to love me always, but now that he hardly ever calls . . ."

Jan looked up, her kind green eyes searching mine. "Julie, I have a friend who loves you all the time. He never forgets to be there when you need to talk."

"Who?"

"Jesus."

I burst into laughter. How silly. Someone I didn't even know loved me? No way.

Thinking about that night, I supposed I should apologize to Jan. I paused, tapping my hairbrush on the palm of my hand as I pondered my own suggestion. Brushing again with a vengeance, I decided to apologize later. I had school to think about now, and so I put the whole thing on a shelf in the back closet of my mind.

I did a good job of forgetting. Stephanie waited for me at the corner. "Why so glum?" I asked cheerfully.

Stephanie heaved a loud sigh as we trudged our way in the leftover summer heat. "The first day of school must be the worst day of the year."

"Almost," I answered, fanning myself with my new spiral notebook. "There's only one day that could possibly rate lower."

"When's that?"

I held my breath a moment for effect, then let the word escape: "Finals."

"You got it." She began to laugh. "How could I forget?"

With Kyle gone, our conversation again flowed with the ease of the "old days."

We found seats in homeroom together and waited for the teacher to hand out our class schedules for the year.

Jenny Wilkinson sat down near us. "Hi, Stephanie. Hi, Julie. How's Kyle?"

"Fine, I guess. He's only been gone two days."

Turning to Stephanie, I said, "That's at least the tenth person who has asked."

"Don't I know it," she hissed. "No one cares how I feel, only about Kyle."

"Don't get so riled," I zipped back. "You must notice they don't ask about me, either."

Stephanie looked like her mother had just died. All the color had drained from her tanned face. I couldn't understand why she always looked like that when someone mentioned Kyle's name.

"OK, Steph, we'll change the subject," I said gently. "Besides, here comes Mr. Silva."

Mr. Silva mechanically passed out schedules by intoning last names. "Landon, Lathrop, Lewis, Leffingwell . . ."

Stephanie and I were studying her card when Rachael Muñoz, sitting behind me, tapped my shoulder. "You're next," she whispered.

"Madden, Marshall . . ."

I jumped and tripped over my own feet. The class choked back laughter as I grabbed my card, managing a more graceful return.

"What classes do you have?" Stephanie asked eagerly.

I whispered back, "English lit., government (ick! and with Mr. Silva, no less), math, PE, and Spanish."

"Great, we have first and third periods together."

"Yeah, much better than last year." I jumped as

the end-of-class bell sounded. "I'd better get used to that again."

"What are you doing after school?" Stephanie asked on our way to class. "Would you like to come over for awhile?"

"Thanks, Steph, but I've been so tired lately I think I'll go home and take a little nap."

"A nap? Are you serious?"

I just nodded. Sometimes I hated to be teased, especially about something that was already embarrassing. I tried to distract her. "I'm glad school begins on Wednesday. It sure makes the week go faster."

"A *nap?*" Stephanie repeated, tossing her golden hair. I hadn't fooled her at all.

After school I gave the message to Tammy that I would be in my room under the influence of my stereo earphones should Kyle call. Then I disappeared into my seclusion, listening to our song as I fell asleep.

"Julie, Julie. Wake up."

The tape had ended, and I looked up to see my mom tapping her finger on one earphone. "Is it Kyle?" I asked quickly, pulling the earphones off and reaching across my bed toward the phone.

"No, it's dinnertime. Now come on, sleepyhead."

Mom's kindness didn't continue the rest of the week as she continually had to wake me up for dinner and hassle me for not doing my daily chores.

I felt bad that I fell asleep so much. But I was so tired that I couldn't help it. I figured the new routine of school was throwing my system off.

Each night after dinner as I did my homework, I flew to the telephone the moment it started to ring. I always answered in my sexiest voice, hoping to hear Kyle's in return—but each time left me filled with disappointment.

By Sunday night I was wild with tension and impatience. I wanted desperately to call Kyle, but now that his long-distance number would show up on the bill, I couldn't sneak away from my old-fashioned, never-call-a-boy daddy as I used to, to phone him.

I tried not to think about the ache inside that I felt for Kyle. As I crawled into bed, I sighed. At least in school I would be able to distract my thoughts more easily.

Monday morning I dragged myself out of bed only twenty minutes before I had to meet Stephanie for school. Getting up to use the bathroom twice during the night was disrupting my sleep immensely.

I grabbed a piece of toast for breakfast, not having time or appetite for much else. I ran out the door and up to the corner.

"I was ready to give up on you," Stephanie called before I had reached her.

"I'm sorry. I overslept," I answered, still a little groggy.

"I've noticed you look a little uneasy during math. Are you sleepy then, too, or having trouble with the work?"

Swallowing the last bite of toast, I wiped my mouth and answered, "No. I've been feeling a little sick to my stomach. I guess, since it's right before lunch, my empty stomach makes me nauseous."

I didn't tell her that the math-class sensation really bothered me. I knew I'd never liked math before, but this semester was beginning quite strangely. Every day in class I got the incredible urge to throw up. I would chew gum, pant gently through my mouth—anything until the feeling passed. It didn't happen in any other class, either.

The only other time I got the same feeling was if I or anyone around me ate tuna. Just the smell of the stuff made me feel so sick I had to leave the area. The thing I couldn't understand, though, was that I had always adored tuna. But now . . .

I shook my head, not even having the energy to think about it.

As Stephanie and I arrived at school, people began asking about Kyle again. I was too embarrassed to say I hadn't talked to him since he'd left, so I would answer, "He's fine."

Stephanie looked at me after about the fourth

questioner had left. "How can you say, 'He's fine'?" her voice mimicked mine. "You haven't even heard from the creep."

The tone of her voice shook me deep inside. She wasn't directing her anger at me but at Kyle. I supposed she didn't ask her question for me to answer it, so I remained silent. Then she muttered, "Is this going to be the pattern for the first day of every week?"

We said nothing more and didn't even pass notes in class. I waved good-bye and threw in a smile before heading off to government. I knew things would be OK when a weak smile touched her lips and crept into her eyes.

As I sat in class I began to feel uneasy again. My bladder felt like it was about to explode. The feeling grew despite my efforts to ignore it and listen to Mr. Silva.

"Does anyone here like school?" a vibrant Mr. Silva questioned.

No answer.

"Come on. School is a fun way to gain the education needed to meet the growing demands of the world. The future is yours, and you must have the education to properly deal with that future to give an excellent world to your children."

I squirmed in my seat. My hand fluttered in the air like a butterfly.

"Yes, Miss Marshall. *You* like to meet the challenge of education head-on?"

I gulped. "Well, uh, Mr. Silva, I guess so . . . but I need to use the bathroom."

Mr. Silva's face flushed as the class tittered. "Of course, Miss Marshall. You may be excused."

"Now class, how can we . . ." Mr. Silva's voice faded as I almost ran down the hall.

I couldn't understand why I couldn't seem to make it through a simple couple of classes without going to the bathroom. I'd developed a new habit of going there between each class period. When I skipped that detour, I'd find myself fighting the desperate need to excuse myself during class.

My friends were even noticing my problem.

"Hey, Julie, are you thinking of buying the john?"

"You spend more time in the hole than you do in class."

"Come on, Marshall, you can't get an A in bathroom attendance."

Even Stephanie joked until I told her I had been having cramps for a couple of weeks and expected my period anytime. Of course, cramps were a normal part of my life as a "woman." And while going to the bathroom every hour wasn't something I was used to, I figured since the cramps were getting stronger and more painful and lasting longer, that maybe they were increasing my need for the trips to the tile cave.

Whatever the reason, it was getting old. Fast.

That morning Stephanie and I met for break.

We had long ago set up a routine of devouring cinnamon rolls every day at the morning break. So we planted ourselves at a table, pulling pieces of the warm sweet bread and popping them into our mouths.

Stephanie shook her hair back from her face. "Julie, why is your mom putting a weeknight curfew on you?"

"She says if I'm too tired to do chores or homework before dinner, then I can stay home and do them after dinner."

"It doesn't seem quite fair."

I shrugged my shoulders. "It's OK. I'm so tired anyway that I really don't care. I figure when I adjust to school, then I'll fight for my rights."

"You can't go anywhere?" she asked, shifting on the bench.

"Nope. Not even to baby-sit for Jan. I have to be in bed by nine-thirty."

"At least your mom doesn't know about the naps you take in class," Stephanie teased.

"Don't laugh. Sometimes I really do find myself dozing in class, too."

We finished our cinnamon rolls and headed toward a group of friends.

"How's your PE class?" Stephanie asked. "You're playing volleyball, aren't you?"

"Yes, and I love it. That's my trophy sport, remember?" I grabbed her arm just a short distance from our friends. Lowering my voice I said, "I hate the days just before my period."

"Why?"

"All the discomfort." Stephanie nodded as I explained. "Like my breasts. The nipples are real tender. They hurt a lot when I run or jump during the game. I feel like I'm going through puberty again."

"Maybe your chest has finally decided to follow your mother's genes instead of your father's," she quipped.

Letting her arm loose, I joined the group. "Thanks a heap," I shot over my shoulder to her.

That afternoon I felt that I had no sooner curled up on my bed when Tammy lifted one of the earphones and stated, "Kyle wants to talk to you," then marched off.

Shaking my head, trying to awaken my sleepy brain, I wearily rolled over and lifted the receiver. "Hi, babe," I muttered.

"Well, hello, sweet babe. You sound like you've been dragged through the woods."

"Yeah. I mean, no. I've been asleep."

"Asleep! In the middle of the day?"

"Yeah," I said, yawning. "It's been real strange. I'm so sleepy all the time. I take a nap every day after school."

"School's too rough on you, huh?"

"Not really. That's what I don't understand." Waking up a little more, I asked, "Why haven't you called?" It was more of a plea than an accusation.

"Oh, you know how busy the first week of school is."

"I never thought of the first week as busy." I allowed my hurt feelings to come across.

"My, aren't we snippy today," Kyle said, laughing softly. I grinned as I listened to his smooth voice. What a way Kyle had of easing away my tension. Then he said, "OK, no excuses. And I'm sorry. Now, how's school?"

"OK, I suppose. Except government. I could live without that." Then I quickly asked, "When do I get to see you again?"

Kyle paused for a long time, and I knew I had said the wrong thing. In a strained voice he answered, "I don't know. . . ."

I tried again. "Kyle, I miss you."

"Yeah . . . I'll call you on Thursday. Bye."

"Kyle, wait—" But he had already hung up the phone. His attitude left me pensive. I felt emptier than before he called. I sat on the floor, hugging my knees and dropping my head to rest on them. Crying didn't help much, but I couldn't stop myself.

The phone rang, and I jumped to answer it, hoping Kyle had decided to call back. "Hello," I said expectantly.

"Well, hello there. What are you so excited about?"

My joy crashed on the floor, and I began to cry silently again.

"Julie, are you there?"

As best I could, I answered, "Yeah, Jan, I'm here."

"What's wrong?"

"Kyle just called. . . ."

"That should make you happy."

"I know, but it didn't. I feel worse than before he called. All we said was hello and good-bye and that I wouldn't see him for awhile."

"I'm sorry, Julie. Would it help for you to come over?"

"No, I'll be OK."

"I'm calling to ask if you want to baby-sit for Stevie on Saturday night."

"You mean you aren't mad?"

"About what?"

"Me laughing at what you said about Jesus," I said hesitantly.

"Of course not."

"I wanted to apologize. . . ."

"There's no need to. Can you sit? Rick is taking me to the Smokehouse Inn for dinner."

"Oooh, how nice. I'd love to. What time?"

"Be here at 5:30?"

"Sure."

"Are you sure you're OK?" Jan's voice sounded concerned.

"Oh, I don't know. I have been feeling so weird lately." Then my words began to tumble out, almost of their own accord. "I sleep a lot, have cramps like I'm going to start my period, only worse. I eat like a pig, I can't eat tuna, I go to the bathroom every hour and at least twice during the night. Math makes me sick, literally. I cry one minute, laugh the next, and have head-aches in between." For the first time, I had thrown all my complaints together. Suddenly I wished I could stuff the words back into my mouth. How could I be so stupid? I stopped, not knowing how to continue. Jan paused for a long, long time. She was so quiet I thought maybe she had left. "Jan? . . ."

Her voice was soft. "Julie, I think you might be pregnant."

I burst in, offended, defensive, and scared. "But I don't have any of the symptoms," I rationalized. "You have to get fat and throw up every morn-ing. But most important, you have to have sex to get pregnant." Then I added quickly, with a false confidence I hoped she wouldn't detect, "I'm sure I'll start my period tomorrow."

I didn't want Jan to have another chance to say anything, so I said, "I'll see you Saturday night. Make sure you have something for Stevie and me to scarf on while you're gone," and I hung up.

Looking in the mirror, I pulled up my shirt and looked at my belly. Front and side views. Nothing looked different. I couldn't . . . but my last period *was* a long time ago. I had my last one right after I met Kyle. Around the beginning of July sometime.

Then reason spoke. *Julie, this is September. You should be having another period. It's been eight weeks.*

I gasped, dropped my shirt, and covered my mouth. Stifling a sob, I whispered, "Oh, Julie, I think you're pregnant."

6

SOMETIMES I hate the night. Suspicions grow into enormous monsters—distorted and threatening. As I would try to fall asleep, I couldn't seem to get comfortable. I'd flip-flop like a fish out of water. When I finally tired of that, I'd lie real still while my mind continued the motion. Fatigue would finally win the battle, and eventually it was morning.

The early sun always chased away the monsters. I would realize my fears were only fantasies and imaginings of my mind. The idea of me being pregnant was ridiculous. Preposterous. I couldn't be. I'd certainly know if I were.

I felt good the next two days, excluding, of course, the minor complaints of my body.

Kyle kept his promise to call on Thursday.

What a sweetie. I now knew not to mention him coming to see me, although my heart ached—no, was dying to ask him to come.

We talked about his school and our families. Chitchat about life's little routines. Then my emotions took charge.

"Kyle, I miss your touch."

"Yeah, sweet babe? I miss yours, too." He chuckled sexily.

My heart warmed. I wanted to touch him, to caress him, but especially to kiss him.

"Are you still there?" he asked.

Softly I replied, "Yes, I'm still here. But I wish I were there."

"Feeling's mutual." He paused for a second. "Listen to our song and think of me, OK?"

"Sure will."

"Bye, sweet babe."

"Bye."

After listening to "I'll Never Leave You" three times, I floated down the stairs to set the table for dinner. Mom's eyes opened wide with unasked questions. I hadn't exactly been Cheri Cheerful lately. But I didn't offer any explanations because I didn't want anything to break the bubble of joy surrounding me.

I slipped into the dining room, taking a stack of plates from the cupboard. I put each one in position, singing quietly. "You are my fantasy, my life, my love. I'll never leave you for another. . . ."

Tammy walked into the room and heard my

song. Her eyes rolled back into her head as she said, "I am so *sick* of that song."

I simply smiled and sang a little louder, "You are the one forever and today. You are the one for always. . . ."

Tammy stuffed her fingers in her ears and made a hasty exit.

The song kept on in my heart even after dinner had begun. I felt happy, listening to the flow of conversation around the table. Nothing could get me down.

"Dinner sure is good, Mom," I said enthusiastically. I spooned another pile of green beans onto my plate. Everything suddenly became quiet. I looked up to discover the reason for the unusual silence. Everyone was staring at me incredulously.

"What are you all looking at?" I asked.

"We aren't used to seeing you eat that much, Julie," Mom said in awe.

"What much?"

"Three helpings, to be exact. Of everything."

"What's wrong with three helpings? Matt eats at least four at every meal."

"Yes, but your brother is a growing boy. He's supposed to eat a lot."

"If growing sons can eat a lot, why not growing daughters?" I asked, shoveling another bite into my mouth.

Dad finally spoke up. "When barely-one-helping Julie begins to eat three helpings, we get curious, that's all."

I shrugged without missing a bite.

"I'm only warning you that you've got to cut down on all that food," Mom said sarcastically, "unless you're hinting for a whole new wardrobe. Two sizes larger."

Her words set my mind to work. My pants *were* beginning to get a little tight. I often unzipped my jeans when I sat down. I had even worn dresses to school the last couple of days to be more comfortable.

During the summer, Mom had said if I wasn't careful, I would get fat from all the ice-cream cones Kyle was giving me. . . .

I put my fork down, not hungry anymore. Fear chased away my appetite, filling my stomach. Fear that Kyle's "ice cream" really *had* made me fat. And the other night Jan had suggested the same thing. As the thoughts shot around inside my head, I knew I had to find out. An idea burrowed its way into my mind.

"Mom, don't forget I have to baby-sit for Jan Saturday night."

"I hadn't forgotten. I will need your help cleaning the house before you go."

"OK. Do you mind if we do it in the afternoon? I'd like to go to the library in the morning to study."

"Go ahead. Plan to be home by noon."

I nodded, then excused myself.

Fear nestled deeper and deeper inside me. I could only sleep restlessly. Friday finally appeared,

holding an eternity of questions that I hoped
would be answered soon.

Saturday brought no change of heart, only a
change of scenery. Even the peace of the library
couldn't dispel the fear growing inside me. I
approached the computer catalog and typed in
the word *pregnancy*. Oh man! There had to be a
couple of hundred books on the subject.

The number 612 appeared most often for the
books on pregnancy. The other books dealt with
subjects related to pregnancy: birth, nutrition, par-
enthood, and sexuality.

I walked up and down the canyons of books,
peering around the corners, hoping no one
would be anywhere near the section dealing
with pregnancy.

"May I help you?" A soft voice surprised me
from behind.

I thought for sure the librarian could hear my
heart thumping as I stuttered, "Uh, no. No,
thanks. Here's what I'm looking for." I pointed
to a section of books which turned out to be
medieval history.

She nodded and walked away.

I waited until she had returned to her desk
before continuing my search.

The first book I pulled from the shelf was a
large thick one entitled *Pregnancy*. I read the
chapter titles, flipped through it, and looked in
the index. The only symptoms it spoke of were
"increased blood supply" and "softening of the

uterus." Disgusting. All technical stuff. I didn't care about increasing blood supplies or what my uterus was up to. I only wanted to find out if I was pregnant.

The second book was just as thick, but at least one chapter sounded promising: "Maybe You Are Pregnant." It, too, had more words than I cared to read, most of them big, long, thick ones, creeping across the pages like fuzzy caterpillars.

I decided to give up. This whole fiasco took at least an hour and a half. People continually walked down the aisle, and I would have to hide the book under my notebook. I'd never realized what a busy place the library is.

There had to be another way to find out.

I worked like a whirlwind for Mom when I got home. I knew if I worked fast and hard, I wouldn't think about all the ifs plaguing me.

The ifs chased me all the way to Jan's house. Her face smiled a greeting, but her green eyes showed concern. She said nothing about our conversation on Monday, yet she must have sensed the questions lurking in the corners of my mind.

"Julie, after Stevie goes to bed, if you'd like, you are welcome to look at the books we have. There are quite a variety of subjects there. You might find something interesting."

Our eyes locked in silent understanding.

"Thanks," I said with more enthusiasm than necessary.

I felt guilty about putting Stevie to bed early,

but my eagerness to see Jan's books enveloped me. I ran my fingers along the binders, looking for anything promising. Two titles caught my eye, and I hesitantly put a finger on top of each book, then slid them out.

Neither helped much. Discouragement filled my heart as I replaced them on the shelves. Both spoke of dealing with morning sickness, constipation, and frequency of urination.

So what about all the other symptoms that attacked *me* daily? Were they connected to pregnancy?

"Oh, help," I said aloud.

I sat crosslegged on the floor, staring dubiously at the shelves. Another book caught my eye: *Family Medical Encyclopedia*. Why not? I grabbed it and turned to the table of contents. Pregnancy, chapter eight.

I read and reread the section on body changes. They listed the same symptoms as the other books, but added breast changes and tiredness.

Going back to the beginning of the chapter, I started to read everything on the subject. I had to use Jan's dictionary to look up many of the words. As I read, the things I learned in health class last year took shape. I began to understand what the teacher had tried to explain to a class of blushing, giggling nitwits.

The thing that surprised me most was that conception, when pregnancy begins (I had to look that one up), happened two weeks follow-

ing your period. Usually. I'd always thought mid-
month was the safe time when you couldn't get
pregnant.

The book also discussed pregnancy tests sold
in drugstores. It said anyone could buy them, and
you didn't need a prescription. A home test. I hit
my head with my hand. Of course! I'd seen all
those goofy commercials with couples waiting to
see if the line was blue or pink! Why hadn't I
thought of that before? A home test would be
perfect. No one would know about my possible
pregnancy but me.

Jan took me home that night. We didn't say
much, and when we got to my house, Jan's eyes
were smiling again. She looked at me and said
earnestly, "No matter what happens to you, I
want you to know I care." I looked away as she
continued, "Jesus is also waiting to help you."

I nodded as if I knew what she was talking
about. "Bye," I muttered, slipping from the car.

• • •

Monday passed as slowly and grouchily as Friday.
Poor Stephanie. She continually tried to cheer
me up. I didn't hear her most of the time, but I
nodded as though I was paying attention.

After school I walked by the drugstore twice.
Then, taking a deep breath, I pushed open the
door. A bell tinkled, signaling everyone inside to
look at me. I painted on my best smile, quickly
scanning the area for any acquaintances. No

familiar faces caught my eye, but to be safe I headed first for the greeting cards. I took my time browsing, all the while checking out every person in the store. I randomly chose a couple of cards as a cover.

Slowly I made my way to the feminine hygiene section. I always hated to go there anyway, but my purpose this time caused me to be extra embarrassed, extra cautious.

It took me a moment to find the pregnancy-test kits. I didn't know what to look for and was surprised to see how small the boxes were and the strange names on them. Confirm, Fact Plus, Answer, and EPT were only some of them. Each cost ten dollars or more. I shoved the greeting cards under my arm as I reached for the first box and began to read it. I shifted my weight from side to side, so nervous I could hardly see the words.

Just then, someone came down the aisle. Panicking, I shoved the box back on the shelf and reached for a box of minipads, pretending to be engrossed in the detail written there.

The woman paid no attention to me and finally left. As I replaced the box of minipads, I noticed a brochure telling in more detail about one of the pregnancy tests. I shoved it into my purse and headed for the cashier. As I opened my purse to produce change for the greeting cards, I realized the pamphlet was in full view. I feigned searching for change as I shoved the pamphlet deep into my purse.

Muttering an obscure thank-you, I grabbed my package and burst outside into the hot sunshine. I walked to my favorite hideaway in a nearby alley, hid in a shadow, and leaned against the cool brick building. I pulled the pamphlet from my purse, reading each word carefully. It said the test would be accurate the first day your period didn't show up. Three drops of urine were to be put in a plastic test case they provided. Within two to three minutes, you have your answer.

I groaned. Sure, it was simple, but ten dollars? The amount stuck in my mind. Where would I get ten dollars? I didn't have anyone to borrow it from. Besides that, how would I buy it without anyone seeing? Where would I hide it at home? No, a home pregnancy test was out. I would have to choose a different alternative.

I ripped up the pamphlet, letting the pieces scatter in the breeze. I didn't think I could make myself go back into that store and buy one of the tests. It was too nerve-wracking! What if someone saw me? Or what if Mom saw the box in the trash after I used the test, or if she came in while I was using it! I shook my head and leaned back against the wall again, searching the sky as if I would find the answer there.

I remembered Jan's book also spoke of pregnancy testing done in clinics and that some of them were free. I went to the library again to use their phone book.

I flipped to the heading "Clinics" in the yellow pages. There were about five listed. I chose a Family Planning Clinic located in the next town. I couldn't risk the chance of being seen at the one in our town.

I wrote down only the phone number, tucking it into the hiding place in my wallet. I walked a long time before finding a phone booth in an area that didn't have people milling about. I took the number out, and my shaking fingers put a coin in the slot.

I waited what seemed an eternity for someone to answer. "Family Planning Clinic," a cheerful voice rang out.

"Umm, I, uh, wondered about, um, a pregnancy test."

The woman's voice never faltered. "Certainly. We have an available opening tomorrow morning. Is eight-forty-five OK for you?"

"Yes, I guess so."

"See you tomorrow."

"Yeah," I said as she hung up.

Fear tightened its grip on my heart as I reluctantly headed for home.

7

I'D read in one of the books on pregnancy that a pregnancy test is most accurate if you use your first urine of the morning. Gross. But I decided I wanted to be sure, so I figured my best bet was to take some with me.

I knew Mom saved everything from Cool Whip bowls to ribbons from packages. I went to her stash in the garage and found a small mustard jar. I washed it on the sly, then hid it in my underwear drawer.

I set the alarm for 6 A.M. and spent the rest of the night checking the clock every half hour or so. I didn't want to miss the chance to get to the bathroom and secretly urinate in the jar.

Everything went smoothly until I returned to my room. I hadn't thought about how to transport the jar, unseen, to the clinic.

The possibilities weren't too promising. I didn't care to share my lunch sack with a leaky jar. Nor did I enjoy the thought of any spilling into my purse. Eau de Urine is not my favorite scent to carry around with me.

I decided to put the jar into two plastic bags, then a brown bag for cover.

Thirty minutes before Mom needed to leave for work, I went to her. I crouched over, walking slowly, twisting my face into one of obvious pain.

"Mom, I've got real bad cramps," I lied. "Can you have Mrs. Anderson take you to work? When I get to feeling better, I can drive to school."

She looked at me a moment and sighed. "I guess so."

She pulled a heating pad from her cupboard. "Use this until you feel better."

"Thanks," I said in a painful tone. I handed her a paper and pen. "Better write me an excuse for school."

She nodded, scribbling her message.

"Bye, Mom." I kissed her cheek and walked slowly to my bedroom. I plugged in the heating pad and curled up on the bed. I wanted to be ready in case she decided to check on me before she left.

I could hear her muffled voice talking on the phone. As soon as I heard the strange car pull up, the front door slammed. I jumped out of bed and got dressed.

The minute I got the car started, I turned the radio on, adjusting the tuner to KBAY.

The ear-filling roar flooded my brain with music, allowing no chance for thoughts to sneak their way in.

Then, without warning, a familiar tune filled the car. "You are my fantasy. . . ." My heart leapt in my chest as my stomach turned upside down. Catching my breath, I turned the radio off as though it had sent fire through the car.

Thankfully, the sign ahead proclaimed Family Planning Clinic. I bit my quivering lip as I pulled into a parking space, then paused a moment, gazing at the ugly, old, block-shaped concrete building before me.

Determined, I stuffed the brown bag into my purse and walked up the cracked cement steps to a large wooden door.

I stepped into the sunlit room and glanced around. I stared at the ugly green-and-white speckled linoleum. Pockmarks evidenced years of chairs scraping across the floor. The chairs that now were set in a semicircle were different sizes and styles. A couple were already occupied by unhappy-looking girls.

Although old, the room was spotless. It smelled of old paint and the musk of freshly watered plants. The receptionist smiled as she took my first name. "It will be about fifteen minutes. Go ahead and sit down." She nodded her head toward the group of chairs.

I thanked her and headed for the chair furthest from the other waiting girls. It commanded a view of all sides of the room. I sat gently on the black leatherette, clutching my purse tightly as though the jar within contained gold.

Short dark hair framed the face of the girl opposite me. Her leg bounced up and down frantically. One hand held a magazine as she chewed the nails of the other.

I fanned myself gently with a magazine I had found in the chair next to me. I glanced at the girl seated to my left.

She continually stared at the ground, pulling her sweater tighter around her trembling figure. Just looking at her caused the warm room to feel hot. I fanned more quickly and noticed my leg, too, bounced an uneasy rhythm.

A woman dressed in Levi's and a light-blue blouse came out of a door and called a name. The girl with jagged fingernails jumped up from her chair.

About ten minutes had passed when the girl returned, and a smile had changed her expression from one of despair to one of relief. She held a flat, oval plastic case in her hand. Her step seemed remarkably lighter than when she had gone in.

Another name was called, and the cold girl with the blank stare jumped as if she had been poked in the ribs. She looked up questioningly, then dragged her feet as she followed the woman in Levi's.

As soon as she left, a couple more woman entered the front door. They seemed much older than I. One of the women smiled at me, but I turned away just like I didn't see her.

The inner door opened again, revealing a young woman in her late twenties. She, too, wore jeans with a casual, Hawaiian-print shirt. She ran her fingers through her long blonde hair as she looked at a card in her hand. "Julie."

I tried to walk confidently to the door. As we entered, we passed the girl with the blank stare. Only now her eyes were red, and her face smudged with running makeup. She pulled her sweater around her little figure and entered a door marked Counseling.

The woman I was following glanced over her shoulder and introduced herself. "Hi, Julie. My name is Ann. My office is right down here."

"I brought some urine from first thing this morning—you know, so it would be more accurate," I told her, taking my sack from my purse.

"It doesn't really matter anymore," she said. "Any time of day is fine, really."

I felt myself blush.

"It's OK," she said as she led me into her office. "Since you have it, we'll go ahead and use it."

Ann's office was small. A white metal cabinet sat in one corner, dwarfed by the old and massive walnut desk in the center of the room. Ann motioned me to a large wooden chair on one side of the desk. She reached into her creaking file cabinet and pulled out a few papers.

"OK, Julie, we need to ask some questions before we do the test. Everything is confidential, but we do need accurate information. Fair?"

I nodded again.

"Date of birth?"

"January twenty-first."

"Age now?"

"Sixteen."

"Have you had any previous pregnancies?"

"No."

"When was your last menstrual period?"

I thought for a while, trying to remember. I knew I had one the first week or two after I met Kyle. That would have to be . . . "Around July eleventh."

"Were you using any form of birth control?"

"No."

Her eyebrows raised with a questioning pause. "Julie," she asked gently, "why didn't you use birth control? At the very least, why didn't you protect yourself from AIDS?"

I wanted to feel uncomfortable telling this stranger about my sex life when I hadn't told Stephanie or even Jan. But her question came so easily, like it was as common as talking about the weather.

I took a deep breath and let the words tumble

in a pile. "Well, I never even thought of AIDS because only gays and people like that get it. Kids don't get AIDS unless they're born with it. And I knew you couldn't get pregnant the first time, and since my periods are so irregular . . . I mean, sometimes I go for two or three months between. So I thought I couldn't get pregnant very easily. Besides, I didn't know what I could use or where to get it."

Ann folded her hands, resting them on the desk. "Julie, anyone who has sex is able to get AIDS. Or any of the other STDs. Do you know about HPV?"

I shook my head.

"Most people don't. It's the most common sexually transmitted organism in the entire U.S. It causes some terrible complications, and it's connected with genital cancer in both sexes. In fact, cancers associated with HPV can and do kill more women every year than AIDS."

I didn't know what to say. It all sounded so scary and terrible. I just couldn't believe any of that could have happened to me. *Yeah, right,* a little voice said inside, *just like you couldn't believe you'd get pregnant.* I swallowed hard.

"Then there's herpes," Ann said.

"I've heard of that."

"Do you know there is no cure for herpes? It ranges from being a mildly irritating recurring disease to being a major, painful problem."

I shook my head again. My heart beat faster as

she listed off more diseases: chlamydia, gonor-
rhea, syphilis. I knew about some, but not that
they were becoming resistant to the treatments
doctors had always used against them. And not
that they could affect my life forever. My stomach moved, and I felt like I might get sick.

"Condoms are crucial to protection from
these diseases, but even condoms cannot guaran-
tee you will not catch any of them."

"It all sounds so horrible."

"It can be. And on top of all that, you *can* get
pregnant the first time you have sex. All irregular
periods do is make it difficult to know when you
ovulate, meaning the time when it is possible to
get pregnant. Irregular periods definitely do not
mean you can't get pregnant. Before you leave
today we will help you decide which method of
birth control would be best for you from now
on. Whatever we choose, we'll include condoms
as protection against AIDS and other STDs."

I looked down at my lap and said quietly, "I
don't expect to have sex again."

"Most girls don't. But sometimes, when the situation comes up, it is hard to refuse. Birth control is very important. It is better to be protected
than pregnant."

I didn't really want any birth control, but now
she had aroused my curiosity. "What kind of
stuff is there?"

"First there are the drugstore varieties, available right off the shelf, even in some super-

markets or department stores." She ticked off on her fingers, "Foam, jellies, creams, condoms, sponges, and suppositories. All of these must be used immediately before intercourse."

I interrupted, "I'm sorry to be so dumb, but what's intercourse?"

"That is the actual putting the penis into the vagina. You aren't dumb. Many people don't know the meaning of the word.

"Back to birth control. Second are the pre-scription methods." She began to tick off on her fingers again. "Norplant is a long-term method where capsules are injected into the upper arm. Depo-Provera is a shot. Neither of these meth-ods is suitable for teens, though.

"The pill is the easiest method. One pill is taken every day for twenty-one days with a pause for seven days to allow the period to come. Some varieties of pills have a sugar pill to take during the pause. This way you don't forget to begin the birth control pills again.

"The diaphragm is used along with creams or jellies. It is a small rubber dome which fits over your cervix. It must be fitted to your body by a doctor. You place it into your vagina up to six hours before intercourse, and should not take it out for at least six hours following. Then it must be cleansed well with warm soapy water and replaced into its plastic case until the next time you need it."

"What method is the best?" I asked.

"No method is completely foolproof, except abstaining. After that, the top two are the pill and diaphragm."

There was a pause, and both our eyes trailed to the paper sack I had placed on the desk. "I guess we had better do the test so you can return to school."

I nodded. My eyes followed her over to the metal cabinet where she pulled out a small, white cardboard box. She opened it and took out a flat, plastic thing about five inches by two inches. It looked like a small tray with some paper and plastic over the top. "We call this the reaction unit." She smiled. "A terrible pun if you ask me." She opened my sack and chuckled softly at the sight of the mustard jar.

I watched as she took a couple of drops of my urine from the jar. "Is that all you need?" I asked.

"That's it."

My face flushed. I had brought the jar half full, and Ann only used a couple of drops.

She placed the drops of urine in a receptacle on the reaction unit. She pushed it in and held it as she looked at the clock.

"There is a hormone secreted by pregnant women from the placenta called HCG. This little test adds HCG antibodies to the urine. If there is any HCG present, they will combine with a chemical to turn the line blue. It will look like a plus sign."

"How long do we wait?"

"About another thirty seconds. Two minutes in all."

I rubbed my palms together, then on the legs of my pants. We both stared at the clock as the second hand crept around the dial. My heart moved farther and farther into my throat as it beat faster and faster. Two minutes. I looked at Ann, afraid to look at the unit in her hand.

"Julie," she said as she placed the reaction unit on the desk. "You are definitely pregnant."

I took a deep breath and looked. A plus sign, dark blue, stood out as clear as could be. There was no doubt.

Ann's voice was soft and understanding. "What do you think you will do about this pregnancy?"

"I . . . I don't know. I guess I never really thought. . . ." I looked at her imploringly.

Ann sighed deeply, her saddened blue eyes piercing mine. "You are not alone. No one ever thinks it could happen to them. It is hard for a girl to admit she is pregnant." Her tone grew softer. "But you *are*. You *must* realize the pregnancy will not go away by itself." Her brows scrunched down, crouching over suddenly stern eyes. "Nor will it go away by hiking, running, jumping, or other hard physical activity. Abortion is the quickest, easiest way to get rid of an unwanted pregnancy. We hope to have simpler methods in the future. But this is all we have right now."

She paused, probably expecting me to speak, but what could I say? My deepest fear had been handed to me with a small, blue plus sign.

Opening a drawer of her desk, she withdrew a pamphlet. She tapped it on the desk as she continued.

"If you want to have an abortion, we can arrange it for you. There are clinics in San Francisco or Oakland that we recommend. But you must remember, the sooner you have an abortion, the safer the procedure will be."

I nodded occasionally, not really hearing anything she said. She placed the pamphlet in my hand as she led me to the door.

"Do you want me to make an appointment for an abortion for you?"

I shook my head. I wanted to get out of this nightmare and back to the real world. If it still existed. "Thanks." I could hardly speak.

As I went out the door, I passed another young woman, who eyed me carefully. I turned my face, shaking my head slightly to allow a curtain of hair to fall between us.

In the privacy of the car I opened my hand to look at the crumpled pamphlet lying there. The letters looked at me boldly. *Abortion: Every Woman's Choice.* I read each word, trying to absorb everything it said. I then ripped the evidence into tiny pieces and flung them out the window. I dropped my head onto the steering wheel for a few minutes.

Looking up, the world was blurry. I wiped my

eyes gently underneath, so I wouldn't smudge my makeup. I pushed my hair behind my ear and set my mind to the task of driving.

I arrived at school much later than I had expected. I crept quietly into government, noticing Mr. Silva's stern eye upon me as I took my seat.

The moment class let out, I ran out the door, pretending not to hear Mr. Silva's call: "Miss Marshall, Miss Marshall."

I could swear the day was shrouded in a hazy fog. Yet the sun continually warmed everything except my insides. I understood why the girl at the clinic had worn a sweater.

"Are you in there, Julie?" Stephanie tapped her finger on my head.

I shrugged my shoulders and offered her a ride home. I drove in silence as Steph prodded me with questions about my morning's absence.

Finally I spoke. "I woke up with bad cramps. Sorry I didn't call. Hope you didn't wait for me too long."

"No," she replied with a pout. "I'm glad we have a time limit set in case one of us neglects to call the other."

Stephanie's hurt expression showed she sensed the lies. Yet, thankfully, she drew her lips in a tight line and said no more.

When I dropped my head on my bed that night, I used the pillow to smother the tears I had been withholding all day. I hoped for sleep and didn't care if I never woke up.

8

I sucked in my breath and tried again. No doubt
about it, there was definitely something in there.
The round, hard mound rose up from the soft-
ness surrounding it. I lay still on the bed, trying
to deny the obvious. That small mound, just
above my pubic bone, must be the alien. This was
the little thing that threatened my sanity, my
plans and dreams.

I looked out the window, wanting to curse the
sun. It had no right to shine its warmth into my
room. For two days I had wanted the sky to cry
with me. But no. The sun shone on as though
there was nothing wrong with being unmarried
and pregnant.

I wanted to call and tell Kyle. Yet every time I
picked up the phone, my heart began to beat

quick and hard, seeming to choke my voice.
Even if I could speak, what would I say? In practice I had told him twenty-three different ways.
Each time, I pictured him responding with the
perfect solution. Whatever that was.

I knew whatever he wanted, I'd do. I wanted
more than anything to please him.

I also knew he wouldn't hesitate to drive from
the city to see me, showering me with love and
kisses. Then we would tell my family together.

In my imagination, my sweet voice gently told
Kyle he was going to be a father. So for two days
I sat by the phone waiting, waiting. Then . . .

"Hi, sweet babe! What's going on?"

The tension I had so carefully kept contained
for days suddenly poured out its bitter flavor. "So
why haven't you called all week?"

"Sorry, sweet babe," Kyle brushed it off. "I've
been making decisions about my future. Where
should I apply for college? Should I go out for
football or wrestling while I'm there? You know,
things like that."

I could feel my dark eyes shooting darts. I
pulled on my hair and bristled. "You have
another decision to make about your future."

"What's that, sweet babe?" he said lightly.

Then my anger faded. Tears poured down my
face. "Kyle," I blubbered. "Kyle . . ."

"Come on, Julie," he said in an irritated voice.
"This is costing me money, you know."

Where was the loving concern I had imagined? I began to stammer, "Kyle, I'm . . . I'm . . . pregnant."

The silent pause made me shiver. "You're what?"

"You heard," I whispered hopefully.

"Unfortunately," he snapped.

"So. What are you going to do about it?" I probed.

"What do you mean, what am *I* going to do about it? It's your problem, not mine. Besides, how do I know it's even my brat?"

No words could have hurt me more. "It's yours," I breathed. "I never had sex before you. If you don't believe that, listen to this: I'm probably two months along. That means summer, and you should know summer means you." I stifled a sob.

Kyle's voice became gentle. "I'm sorry, sweet babe. Of course it's mine. You just took me by surprise, that's all."

I asked my question again, desperately hoping he had the answer. "So, Kyle, what do we do?"

"Well, there's only one thing *to* do. Get rid of it."

"You mean abortion?"

"Of course."

"I don't know, Kyle. I don't know how I feel about abortion."

"Well, you have no other choice."

"I don't know. I just remember last year, a girl from school named Charlene had an abortion. I was so angry with her that I couldn't speak to her for weeks. All I wanted to do was to walk up to her and grab her arms and shake her till her braces fell out, yelling, 'Charlene! How *could* you?'"

"Oh, Julie. Come off it. Don't you realize things are different when it's *you* that's pregnant?" His voice declared impatience.

The words cut into my heart. But of course he was right. Unwillingly, I answered, "OK." Then, I needed to know. "Do you love me?"

With zero tenderness, he said, "That's a silly question. Yes. I love you."

"Will you come to see me soon?"

"I guess."

"You don't sound very promising."

"It's up to the old man, Julie. You know that."

"Yeah."

"Look, I'll try to convince him, OK?"

"I really need to see you, Kyle."

"Hey, I gotta go."

I possessed neither the strength nor the words with which to protest. I just sat there, listening to the click and the final hum of desertion. I put the receiver down firmly, hoping to drown out the sounds of emptiness.

Too confused to cry, I sat numbly staring at the phone, even as it rang again.

In the distance I could hear Tammy's breathless hello, then her pounding feet up the stairs. She banged her fist on my door, calling, "Jan is on the phone."

"I don't want to talk to her."

"So what'll I tell her?"

"What do I care?"

As Tammy bounded back down the stairs, I changed my mind. Swiftly, I lifted the receiver. "Hi, Jan."

Just then Tammy picked up the other end. "Jan—"

"Thanks, Tammy, I got it." I could envision Tammy's confused expression as she hung up the phone.

"Hi, Julie," Jan spoke gently. "I'm calling to see how you are feeling."

I ignored the unasked questions and asked one of my own. "Jan, why can't my life be like yours?"

"What do you mean, Julie?"

"Why don't you ever fall apart when disaster hits you?"

Jan laughed. "Oh, Julie, you've seen me cry lots of times."

"Yeah, but your tears are different," I insisted. "You're always talking about the good things that come out of rotten situations. Your outlook on everything is so . . . well, it's so different from mine."

"My outlook wasn't always so positive."

"Really? What changed you?" I asked, hoping to find a solution to my world of problems.

"It's Jesus, Julie. He has given me a new outlook on life. The problems are still there, but he

gives me the strength to cope with them.
Strength to know he has planned for my best
even through the hard times."

"Oh, lay off that Jesus stuff. Can't you ever talk
without bringing him up?" I knew I should
regret these bitter words, but I didn't.

"I can't quit talking about Jesus any more than
I could quit breathing. He is how I live."

"If your stupid Jesus is so good, they why am I
pregnant?" I blurted. I closed my eyes, my anger
finally expressed and shame coming over me. I
hadn't wanted to tell Jan. I had just wanted to
have the abortion and never let her know. I was
sure that now she wouldn't let me baby-sit for
her anymore, let alone be my friend.

Jan's soothing voice brought me into a shelter
I hadn't known existed. "I thought so. Have you
told your mom?"

"No."

"It might be a good idea."

"Why, what can she do?" I asked sarcastically.

"Mothers are a lot more understanding than
we give them credit for. Maybe she can help
guide your decisions in coping with this."

"I don't need any guidance. I can handle this
myself."

"Can you?" Her voice pressed gently into my
wounds. "Why don't you come over? It would
be easier to talk about it face-to-face."

I had no energy to speak to anyone. I wanted
to skip dinner, crawl into bed, and forget this

whole nightmare. "Maybe another day. I . . . I just don't feel . . ."

"That's OK, Julie. Just remember I'm always here to help, to listen, or just to offer a place for you to get away."

"Thanks," I said, really meaning it. She amazed me. I might as well have slapped her in the face, and still she just talked as if I never said what I did about her "friend."

"I'll be praying for you."

Big deal, I wanted to say. Yet the prospect of God knowing about this mess somehow began to make me feel a bit better. "OK. Bye."

I set the phone back upon the table, curled into a ball, and began to plan the next horrid steps of my life.

. . .

My hands shook as I dialed the number. The receiver continually got wet, and I had to wipe my hands on the bedspread. I tapped my finger nervously.

"Family Planning."

I felt I had lost my voice. "I want to get an abortion," I said hoarsely.

"How far along do you think you are?"

"I was told probably about seven weeks."

"Are you certain this is what you want?"

"Yes."

"I will need your name and phone number. We will get back to you when we have set up an appointment. Do you prefer going to Oakland or San Francisco?"

"Oakland, I guess."

"We will call you to confirm the appointment tomorrow."

"But you can't call here."

"That's fine. You can call us if you prefer."

I sighed. "Yes."

. . .

Days continued to pass slowly and with extreme effort, as though they might not continue to another sunrise.

The clinic had arranged a procedure date a week from Friday. They suggested I arrange for someone to take me. They said the distance was too great for my emotional condition before the abortion and my physical condition after it.

I would have to tell Mom. I'd thought a lot about it. Yes, it would hurt her. But I figured she would be more hurt to discover later that I hadn't asked for her help. Even if her only help is to drive me to some clinic in Oakland.

Too bad there are no books entitled *How to Tell Your Mom You Are Pregnant*. I certainly could have used one.

Sometimes you needed to wear running shoes and carry a bullhorn to tell Mom anything. When she wasn't at work, she was cleaning the house. Anytime I approached her, she put me to work at the opposite end of the house.

Finally one day I became desperate. I knew I had to tell her that day, or I just might explode like an overblown balloon.

Her hair was wrapped in a red gingham bandanna, and she was waving a can of dust spray in one hand and a cloth in the other. You could see her mind running through her list of things to do as she aimed her body for the kitchen. I jumped in front of her, bracing myself in the doorway. Her eyes searched my face curiously.

"Mom, we really need to talk."

"Sure, Julie," she said absently, tucking the can and rag under her arm. "Let's sit down for a snack when we get this mess cleaned up." She pulled my hands down from the doorframe, stuffing them with the spray can and rag. "Go dust the upstairs, would you please? Thanks. I won't forget the snack. We can have ice cream."

She gently pushed me aside as I numbly said, "Sure, Mom." I knew that when the housecleaning was finished, it would be dinnertime. That would be rushed, too, for it was her and Dad's special night out.

My final approach would be tactless and painful, but she left me no alternative. It would have to be after they came home.

I waited nervously on the couch. Dad said his usual gruff hello and kissed me on the cheek. He sauntered upstairs to bed. I grabbed Mom's wrist. "Can we please talk, *now?*"

My pleading suddenly seemed to register on

her face. She sat down, and I wiped my palms on my jeans.

"Mom, remember all the teasing about me getting fat?"

She nodded and jumped to her usual conclusions. "I'm sorry, Julie. We all love you and don't mean to hurt your feelings."

I shook my head in frustration, letting my hair sting my cheeks. *"No,* Mom, you don't understand. Yes, I *am* getting fat. Most girls do when they're pregnant."

Her face turned to shades of disbelief. As tears came to my eyes, she realized this was no cute, little joke. She scanned me silently, searching for proof. Suddenly she burst into tears, putting her head into her hands.

"Mom." I grabbed her arm, trying to pull her hands from her face. "Please don't cry," I pleaded.

"Julie Marie, leave me alone. I don't want to talk to you now." She stumbled up the stairs, leaving me to stare blindly at the telephone commercial on TV.

I sat there wondering if my heart was still beating. My muscles had frozen, and so had everything else. Maybe twenty minutes had passed when I forced myself off the couch to turn off the TV.

When I reached my room, I sat staring in the mirror. This had to be happening to someone else. But the person in the mirror looked like a frightened me.

I could hear muffled sobs and occasional voices drifting through the hallway.

Crawling into bed, I pulled my pillow tight over my ears. I bit my lip, trying desperately not to cry. Slowly a new fear crept inside me. The fear that tomorrow would come.

9

I awoke as Mom lowered herself gently onto the edge of my bed. "Julie," she said softly, touching my shoulder. "Can we talk now?"

I looked at her, turning away quickly when I saw her red-rimmed eyes. Her lids were swollen from crying. "Sure, Mom," I said, frightened by what she might have to say.

"Honey, I'm sorry I couldn't talk to you last night." Her hand dropped from my shoulder to clasp her other tissue-filled hand. "I . . . I wanted to think more about what you had said."

"I don't understand." I plucked at the sheet.

"Can I be honest?"

"I suppose." *Now why would I want her to lie?* I thought.

"I never thought I would be sitting here with you, discussing something like this."

I looked away, ashamed.

"I guess I never thought I would see you in this situation, and that's why I never discussed . . . umm . . . sex before."

I felt as though I were being stripped naked in front of her. Her obvious embarrassment joined mine to make us both uneasy.

"At first I was angry with you. What a little tramp, I thought."

"Mom!" I protested, now facing her.

"Wait, Julie. Then I remembered the relationship your father and I had before we were married. I tried to remember how much I loved him and the way I didn't think much about our actions."

I tried not to look shocked. I had hardly ever thought of Mom and Dad as doing anything more than kissing. I guess that's because that's all we kids ever saw.

"I should have thought about those feelings before," she continued with difficulty. "We never, uh . . . well, I never could have gotten pregnant, but if our engagement had been much longer . . . well, who can say?"

She shook her head as if bringing herself in from a daydream. "I *should* have talked about sex with you. I *should* have told you how to prevent babies."

I nodded slightly. A little information like I

received at the Family Planning Clinic would have helped a lot.

"So after I blamed you, I shifted the blame to myself."

That sounds pretty good, I thought. *Maybe this isn't really my fault after all.*

Mom's sharp words caught my attention. "But I'm *not* to blame, Julie. *You* made the decision to have sex with Kyle. I didn't force you to."

Tears started to fill my eyes as I began to protest softly, "Mom?"

She continued as though I had said nothing. "After a while I blamed Kyle. 'It must be his fault,' I reasoned. 'He forced Julie into this.'"

"Mom, no one forced me into anything."

She sighed. "I know. . . ." Her voice trailed off. "Julie, we all bear some blame. We share the guilt. Me, for not guiding you as a mother should. And you—"

"But Mom, I didn't think I could get pregnant." I suddenly realized how absurd that statement was.

We both said nothing for a moment, then Mom looked toward the door and pleaded, "Why, Julie, *why?*"

"Mom, I'm sorry." Another dumb statement. I was so confused, I didn't know whether I was sorry or not. I didn't know if I was alive or not. I didn't know anything.

Mom interrupted my thoughts. "Over and over I thought that, no matter what, I love you.

Because I love you, I must stand with you, not hide in a corner, not point an accusing finger at anyone."

"Oh, Mom, I love you, too," I blurted. We both burst into fresh tears and gave each other a hug that would have crushed a bear.

Wiping her eyes, Mom said, "What are you going to do?"

I spoke each word separately, as an attempt not to stammer, "I have an appointment for an abortion."

Mom gulped, and I could tell she did not want to face reality any more than I did. "When?"

"Friday."

"So soon," she said to herself.

I spoke up with authority and wobbly confidence. "The sooner the better, and safer," I quoted.

She just looked at me, her reddened eyes full of pain. And perhaps fear?

"Mom, I have to go to Oakland for the abortion. Will you take me?"

She gulped again. "I don't know if I approve of abortion."

I looked at her, not knowing what to say.

As Mom looked into my begging eyes, she said shakily, "I will take you. I disagree with your choice, but I will honor your right to make it."

She shuddered visibly and said, "I hope your father understands."

"Will you tell him for me please, Mama?"

I hadn't called her Mama in years. She understood why I used that special name now. And so she became willing to ease my pain, if only a bit, by telling Dad about my unpopular decision.

I avoided Dad all day. At dinner he could hardly say hello to me. Before being seated, he gave Tammy her customary kiss, and Mom hers. He didn't attempt to complete the tradition I used to hate—to give me one, too.

I missed that kiss, but I understood. I would never again be his little girl. I knew he accepted what had happened but wouldn't talk about it. That's just the way Dad was.

I went to bed early, wanting to avoid all family contact. Even if they didn't cut me off, I had to separate myself. I no longer felt like a part of this respectable family.

It was so strange . . . just a few short weeks ago, I had complained to Jan about how unloving our family was. And now I saw that wasn't true. The love had always been there; I just hadn't seen it.

I tried not to think about what would happen in only a few days. My body would be altered, not to mention my life. But I hoped there would be less alteration than if I carried this alien for another seven months. I wanted to be parted from it as soon as possible.

The easy way out. Not even Stephanie would have to know.

10

"Is this it, Mom?"

"Yes. Are you sure you don't want me to come in?"

I sighed deeply. "Yeah."

"I'll be back in three hours."

"OK."

She stuffed some money into my hand. "It's building E-6."

"Thanks." I turned and began to open the door.

"Julie."

I swung around to face her. "What?"

She wiped tears from her eyes, hesitating. "Bye."

I was pretty sure there had been something more she wanted to say, but she was unable to speak. As she drove away, I felt a sense of loss. A loss of what, I'm not sure.

Turning, I was surprised by the group of buildings in front of me. Instead of the sleazy, run-down, back-alley house that I expected, I saw a fairly large office complex. I wound around the wooden buildings, set among lush, green landscaping. I found E-6 between a dentist's office and a chiropractor's office.

As I pushed open the glass door, a scene of contrasts appeared before me.

The waiting room was large. The tastefully papered walls were decorated with sketches of beautiful, modern women. Soft music filled the air. Couches and chairs lined the walls. Then there was the contrast to all that calm.

People were strewn about. Some male, some female. All waiting. The women's faces were painted with fear, some with shame. The men looked sad, uncomfortable, and sometimes a touch angry. No one spoke.

Next to the door, a man draped his slumbering form across a chair. His arms were folded across his chest, reminiscent of my father before the TV, "watching" football games.

A young girl, maybe even younger than I, rocked back and forth slightly on a chair. She bit one fingernail, her eyes round with emotion. Along with fear and shame, I detected confusion. I wanted to reach out and touch her, but I could barely keep myself together.

As I approached the reception window, a door opened and a name was called. An older woman rose from a couch. Her long, stringy, gray-streaked hair was draped about her face. Her teeth were crooked, stained yellowish brown from the cigarette she hastily extinguished in the ashtray next to the couch.

"Can I help you?" a friendly voice questioned.

I turned to the receptionist. "My name is Julie Marshall. I have an eleven o'clock appointment."

"I have some papers for you to fill out, Julie. Fill in this upper portion here, read these two blue papers, and sign the yellow one stating you have read them."

I nodded as the pleasant young woman handed me three pieces of paper, a clipboard, and a pen. I tried to focus my eyes and understanding on the sheet of instructions, which told what would be happening to me during the next two and a half hours. I finally gave up and signed the papers anyway, returning them to the receptionist.

"That will be three hundred and twenty five dollars, please."

I handed her the cash my mom had given me.

"Would you like something to help you relax?" she asked.

I nodded and she handed me a paper cup of water and a small pill.

I returned to my seat and began to check out what type of woman would seek an abortion. Some were beautiful, some looked like well-used pieces of equipment. Some were heavy, some slender. It was hard to believe each had something in common. Their bodies all harbored an unwanted alien. And nobody wanted that alien to become a person to complicate their lives.

Slowly the realization came over me that I was there for the same reason and purpose.

Suddenly I felt I was drowning in fear. Wave after wave enveloped me. I felt I was fighting for a breath. Even though my eyes were open wide, I could see everything only through a misty haze. Shapes had little color, no names, and dull voices. I gripped the seat of the armless chair and held on.

I bit my bottom lip and closed my eyes tightly. Time wore snail's feet. The only thing that finally penetrated this awesome fear was someone speaking my name.

Somehow I got off the chair and walked toward the voice. I didn't really care who the voice belonged to, I just went.

I barely glanced at the doors we passed as we walked down the hallway. I was led into a bright, clean room. It was furnished with only a sink, work counter, refrigerator, and a couple of chairs. Various equipment, test tubes, and timers lay about the counter. It looked like a lab.

A young, attractive black woman greeted me. "Hi, Julie."

I tried very hard to smile, with no success. "Hi," I said blandly.

"Take this cup and give us a small sample of your urine for a pregnancy test, please."

I nodded as I took the paper cup from her outstretched hand.

It only took a couple of minutes for me to complete my task. My hand shook as I returned the cup to the lab technician. I was weighed, measured for temperature, blood pressure, and pulse rate. Then, the procedure I hated: drawing blood. "What's the blood for?"

"We do a few quick tests on it. Hematocrit, hemoglobin, and Rh factor. If you are Rh negative, we will give you a RhoGAM injection following the procedure."

I nodded as if I knew what she was talking about.

Next, someone took me down another hallway to a room. It had four cubicles with bright sky blue drapes hanging in front of the doorways to offer privacy. Three women dressed in paper gowns sat staring at a table between them. It seemed odd that no one was reading the magazines lying there. Each woman looked up briefly as I entered the room.

"Go into one of the cubicles and remove your clothes. You may leave your socks on, but everything else must come off."

For the first time I glanced at the dark-haired, brown-eyed lady who had led me here. "Why everything?"

"The physician will want to do a breast check before he begins the procedure."

I cringed. No one but Kyle had ever touched my breasts.

"Put your clothes into the small plastic bag you will find in the cubicle," she continued. "You will carry the bag with you throughout your stay here until it is time to put your clothes back on."

I entered the cubicle nearest the door. I undressed slowly, not enjoying the thought of putting on the paper gown. I hate those awful things. I don't understand why the manufacturers insist on leaving in the breeze that seems to come with them.

I picked up a magazine before I sat down in the cold chair. A few minutes had passed when a girl who looked a couple of years older than I approached the entrance to the room. She was given the same undressing instructions, and she nodded confidently with what appeared to be impatience.

After she shed her clothes, she sat next to me. The front of her ash blonde hair had been pulled back with a clip at the crown of her head. Her blue eyes were confident, unlike any of the others in the small room.

She leaned over to me and said, "Hi, my name is Rachel. What's yours?"

"Julie."

"This your first time here?"

I nodded.

"This is my second."

I tried in vain to conceal my shock. Someone would actually go through this more than once?

"Hey, you scared?"

I nodded again.

"Don't be. There's nothin' to it. The worst part is lying on one of those awful tables with your legs spread apart."

"Doesn't it hurt?" I whispered.

"Nah. Not really. It just feels a little like cramps when you get your period."

"What about that machine. Doesn't *it* hurt?"

"Of course not. By then it's almost over. It feels a little like something's being sucked out of you. But big deal. That's what's happening anyway."

"What about after you get home?"

"I felt fine. I bled for a few days. Life returned to normal." She looked down at her stomach. "At least for a while, anyway."

I knew Rachel was trying to be helpful, but instead of soothing my fears, she caused them to grow.

"Your boyfriend know you're here?" Rachel asked, unwrapping a piece of gum.

"Yes."

"What does he think?"

"He's the one who suggested it."

"Of course. They all do."

Offended by her obvious slander of Kyle's reputation, I snapped, "He loves me and wants the best for me."

"Sure, honey, that's why he's here holding your hand."

I opened my mouth twice, but I could think of no good comeback.

"Look," Rachel said, giving my arm a swift pat, "I don't mean to talk nasty about your man. I seem to spit all my venom for my man on everyone else's. But I'm surprised you didn't think of the abortion first."

"I guess because I've never liked the thought of abortion."

She looked amazed. "Then why're you here?"

"Because," I said hesitantly, "my boyfriend wanted it."

She pulled her brows together and scratched her head under the hair clip. Now *I* had left *her* speechless.

I clasped my hands together, dropped my chin to my chest, and closed my eyes. I didn't want to talk anymore. I *wanted* to think, but that was so hard to do.

Why *was* I there? Whose choice was this abortion anyway? No matter how I looked at it, the choice was Kyle's. I hadn't thought much about anything except, Why am *I* pregnant?

Thinking was too hard right now. As long as I was there, I figured I might as well go through with it.

Another name was called, and I realized I was

next. My heartbeat began to increase, and I froze. I suppose if someone were there to take a picture of me right then and show it around, folks would think a corpse had been lifted from its casket and propped in a chair. "This is no mannequin," I could almost hear someone say. "Mannequin faces never show absolute terror such as this."

My morbid daydream was broken by a woman in a marine blue cotton gown. "Julie," she said.

I hesitated, then stood. The floor felt so cold under my feet. I found I had forgotten to leave my socks on. I numbly picked up the plastic bag filled with my clothes.

My insides were quivering like Jell-O as I walked down the hall after her. I followed her through a door marked OR. My eyes scanned the room quickly. Against one wall was a countertop and metal sink. Against another was a bed on wheels fitted with a paper sheet and a pillow. They called it a gurney.

In the center of the room was a strange looking table. It was cushioned and covered with paper. The strange part about it was the size. It was short. Too short for anyone I knew, unless we were discussing an eight-year-old. Extending from each side of the lower end of the table were two metal arms. Each stretched out and up into the air, spreading widely apart. At the top there was what appeared to be a curved metal pipe cut lengthwise.

Beside the table on one side was a thing that

looked like a cabinet on wheels. There were two
jars and a plastic hose sticking out of the top.

Next to the cabinet was a metal tray, also on
wheels. Placed neatly upon it was a row of instru-
ments. Long metal rods that gradually got bigger
caught my eye.

"Up on the table, Julie," the nurse said cheerfully. At that I burst into tears.

The nurse put her arm around me and helped
me to sit on the small stool at the foot of the
examining table. She gently brushed the hair
from my face. "Julie, are you sure you want to go
through with this?"

I could only cry. I couldn't think.

The door opened, and a bearded man walked
in. I tried to draw into myself, afraid of his reaction to my tears.

He approached me, placing a hand on my
shoulder. "You don't want this abortion, do
you?" His tone, kind and soft, calmed me a slight
bit.

I shrugged my shoulders.

"Get up on the examining table, and we'll see
how far along you are."

I obeyed. I understood what Rachel meant
about the embarrassment of lying with my legs
spread apart on that table. My buttocks were all
the way down at the edge of the table. My legs,
high in the air, were supported under my knees
by the metal "pipes."

The doctor slipped a surgical glove onto his

right hand and reached what felt like his whole hand into my vagina. I gasped. It hurt. He told me to relax. If I hadn't been so scared, I probably would have laughed. Funny man! How could anyone relax with a stranger's hand inside of her?

The doctor's other hand pressed on my stomach as he moved his right hand gently about inside me. He turned to the nurse and said, "Nine weeks."

He looked at me and said, "Julie, we won't do the procedure today. You are not emotionally ready to make this decision. You still have three more weeks in which this can be done safely. Go home. Think about it. If you feel you are ready to try again, give us a call."

He slipped off the glove, tossed it into the trash, then patted me on the leg. He washed his hands at the sink and left.

The nurse helped me up and handed me some tissues and my bag of clothes. "Julie, you're on your own now. I must get ready for the next patient."

As I left the OR, I glanced into a room I hadn't noticed on my earlier trip down the hall.

A small sign marked Recovery was posted on the wall beside the door. Inside, a row of gurneys were lined up against the far, windowless wall. A woman draped with a paper sheet occupied each one. All the women were silent. Shock had replaced fear. The alien had been pulled from them. Mine still remained.

An eerie feeling passed over me, and I shuddered visibly. I increased my pace to reach the room of cubicles once more.

Rachel was gone, but I didn't really care. I changed more quickly this time. I was anxious to leave.

The receptionist kindly returned my money. I walked out into the bright sunshine and sat under a tree. I wished I hadn't insisted Mom go shopping instead of waiting around the clinic.

I couldn't control the sobs that came upon me, and I hugged my knees for comfort. "Oh, God, I am so confused," I cried. "What am I going to do? Oh, God. Help me! What am I going to do?"

11

"FORGET it, Julie. Forget it. It's all over."

"But, Kyle!" I pleaded through my tears.

"Look, honey. I told you to get an abortion. If you can't even follow a basic instruction, our relationship is over."

"I love you."

"If you loved me, you would have gotten that abortion."

"I thought you loved me."

"I thought I did, too. I guess we were both mistaken."

"Kyle, I need your help."

"OK. I'll send you two hundred and fifty dollars. That's what I was going to send you for the abortion anyway."

I pulled hard on the hair twisted around my

finger. "Not that kind of help, Kyle. I need *you.*"

"I already told you no, Julie. I've had enough. I want my life to go on without any hassles. And it's obvious you are becoming a big one."

Anger swelled my heart. "What about *my* future, Kyle? Don't you think I'll be hassled?"

"That's your own tough luck, honey. I don't want to hear from you again. Understand?"

"No, I don't understand. And you *will* hear from me again. Good-bye!" For once I wanted to have the last word. I slammed the phone down as hard as I could, hoping he'd get the message.

I turned down dinner and had tears instead. I was so angry and hurt—and so mixed up, too. I didn't understand why my life had to be so bummed. "God, why don't you do something?" I said angrily to the ceiling.

When the tears stopped, I felt like a caged cat. Anxious, restless. My energy was ready to explode. I picked up the phone. I needed help. I needed to talk to someone, someone who loved me.

Jan's line rang again and again.

I hung up and dialed another number. "Is Stephanie there, please?"

I twirled my hair into a perfect ringlet while I waited.

"Yes," Stephanie said breathlessly.

"It's me. Julie. Can you talk?"

"Yeah, sure, Jule. What's up?"

"I've got to tell you, Steph." I began to cry again.

"Hey, Jule, what is it?" Stephanie said softly.

"You've got to promise you won't tell a soul."

"You know I won't, Julie."

"Kyle has broken up with me." Sobs almost concealed my voice.

Stephanie hesitated a moment. "Maybe that's for the best, Julie."

"What do you mean?" I almost screamed. "Some friend and comfort you are."

"I'm sorry, Julie. It's just . . . well, I never thought Kyle was real good for you."

"Oh, what do you know?"

She didn't answer.

"Hey, Stephanie. Look. I'm hurting so bad right now. . . ."

"I bet," she said kindly. After a pause she forced some cheerfulness. "Hey, why don't we go shopping tomorrow?"

"Can't. I have a doctor's appointment."

"Oh yeah? What for?"

I clenched my teeth, closed my eyes, and wondered what I should say.

Stephanie spoke up again. "Which doctor?"

"Dr. Womack."

"I've never heard of him. What kind of doctor is he?"

"An obstetrician."

"A what?"

"A doctor who takes care of pregnant

women." I paused and took a deep breath. "I'm pregnant, Steph."

I heard her gasp and felt myself suddenly grow weak. "Oh . . . so what are you going to do?"

"Go to the doctor's tomorrow."

"Don't be funny. What are you going to do with the baby?"

"I don't know yet."

"Does Kyle know?"

"Why do you think he's breaking up with me?"

"Oh." I could almost see Stephanie fidgeting. I felt it over the phone. Suddenly she said, "Julie, my mom's calling. I'll phone you later."

"OK. Bye." Some help she was. What happened when I needed friends the most? Everyone split. So who was I supposed to turn to? Who could keep me from collapsing?

. . .

Dr. Bowers. Dr. Fetler. Dr. Womack. Obstetrician/Gynecologist Group.

I pulled open the door and let Mom walk in first. She went to the reception window and announced my name. The woman handed her a clipboard with a pen on a ball-chain leash. I felt so dumb. Like a little kid in a doctor's office who couldn't fend for herself.

Mom chose a seat where I would rather not sit. I plopped myself down next to a woman in obvious discomfort. She used her stomach as a tray, resting her crossed arms upon it.

Muzak played over the speakers, and I heard an instrumental version of Madonna's latest song. Not my style. I leaned to complain to Mom, and what was she doing? She was filling out the sheet of paper for me. "Mom, I can do that, thank you. I'm a big girl now."

Mom looked hurt and embarrassed. "I'm sorry, Julie. I wasn't thinking."

She handed me the board with the pen trailing along behind. I got halfway through and had to ask her for some of the answers anyway. They asked who would pay for the bill, the address of Dad's work, and so on.

We were lucky, Mom said, that Dad's insurance would help pay for this pregnancy.

I let Mom return the form to the window, while I pretended to read a magazine. My eyes couldn't focus on the words. I was too interested in all the pregnant women in the large room. I had never in my life seen so many stomachs in various stages of swelling.

I tried to imagine what the women used to look like before their bodies became so disfigured. Then I wondered what I would look like in the future.

Maybe I should have gotten the abortion after all. Did I really want my body to be stretched out of shape like these bodies here?

I was glad to be summoned as Julie Marshall. Not Mrs. Marshall, or worse, Miss Marshall.

Thankful that Mom didn't try to come with me, I self-consciously stepped across the room and slipped inside the door.

I assumed the woman leading me to the scale was a nurse. Her pointed chin, her glasses, and her hair poked into a bun vaguely brought to mind an old fairy tale. I couldn't think of which one.

As I stepped on the scale, I wished I had worn my lighter weight clothes instead of jeans, high-tops, and a heavy sweater.

A paper cup was pushed into my hand. I wondered if I would ever get over the embarrassment of handing someone a cup full of my urine. What's worse, I was informed that from then on, I would need to produce a sample at each of my appointments.

Then I was led to a small, windowless room. One wall had a sink nestled in a countertop. The opposite wall had a door in the center of it.

Once again, in the center of the room, was another one of those funny-looking short tables like they had at the abortion clinic. An inverted metal plate sat on the floor. From the center rose a metal accordion neck from which blossomed a metal bowl with a lightbulb in the middle.

The strange light and a stool were at the foot of the exam table.

The nurse told me to undress in the dressing

room, pointing her chin and finger toward the unopened door. The dressing "room" was smaller than my closet at home. Attached to the wall was a small bench with a mirror placed over it. When I closed the door, there wasn't much room to undress.

Once again, a breezy gown took the place of my clothes. I peeked out the door. The nurse was still there, waiting impatiently.

"Sit here, please." She patted the table.

As I sat, my naked behind immediately stuck to the paper. The nurse put a sheet on my lap.

She checked my blood pressure and pulse. "And why are we here today, Julie?" she asked innocently.

"I'm pregnant," I answered in the same innocent tone.

"Oh? And when was your last menstrual period?"

I got the impression she didn't believe me. "July eleventh."

Her eyebrows rose again as she checked her chart. No doubt to see how old I was, or rather, how young.

Suddenly I remembered the fairy tale. Hansel and Gretel.

She left, and I was not disappointed in the least.

I wanted to snoop around the stuff on the counter. Interesting gadgets and booklets lured my attention. The biggest curiosity was a large, see-through plastic thing with something pink in the middle of it. I suppose it was a uterus. It looked kind of like the pictures they showed us in health class last year.

I was afraid to get off the table. Afraid the paper would go with me wherever I went and afraid the doctor would catch me with my gown open wide in the back, looking at his things.

So instead, I waited in this freezing room forever, or at least twelve hours, before the doctor finally showed up.

In the meantime, I think I learned all the details of his medical schooling. I memorized his little framed documents posted around the room. I felt they could have had something a little more interesting to look at hanging on the walls.

Finally a form came flying into the room with a white coat trailing behind like angels' wings.

"Well, good afternoon, Julie. I'm Dr. Womack. What can I do for you?"

His cheeriness threw me. After the nurse, I expected an old grouch. His balding head reminded me why I was there. "I'm pregnant."

"Well, so you are. When was your last menstrual period?"

I got the feeling he and his nurse ought to get together or that he should have read the chart. "July eleventh."

"How are you feeling?"

"Fine, I guess."

"Good."

It was funny how during the whole time he

was speaking, he made me lie down and began to feel my breasts with icy hands. His chatter helped me to forget what was happening.

"OK, Julie. It's time to take a look." He pushed a button and said into a speaker, "Pam, room three, please."

"Oh no!" I wanted to say. "Do you have to?" The doctor was OK, but that nurse?

The door opened and a young woman entered, her brown hair, which was the same color as mine, curled about her face. "Hi," she said, her eyes cheerful behind her glasses.

"This here's Julie," the doctor said to the nurse.

"Hi, Julie. I'm Pam."

"Hi."

"Julie, you need to scoot all the way down to the bottom of the table so Doctor can examine you."

Eager to please them both, I scooted down, almost too far.

The doctor picked up a thing that looked like a cross between a metal duckbill and a clamp. "What is that?"

Dr. Womack laughed. "This here cold thing is called a speculum. It opens up your vagina so I can get a good look at your cervix. The cervix is the neck of your womb, which sticks out into your vagina."

"You're right, it's cold," I said as he put it in. "Isn't anything warm in this office?" I said sarcastically, feeling a bit like my usual self.

"Hey, Pam, looks like we've got a sassy one here." Pam gave me a wink. "OK now, Julie," the doctor continued in a serious tone. "I am going to take a mucous sample from your cervix for what is called a pap smear."

"A pap smear?" I questioned.

"It's a simple test to check for cervical cancer."

"You don't think I have cancer, do you?"

"Probably not. But I can't know unless I do the test."

"Aren't I too young to have that kind of cancer?" It sounded so much like a woman's disease, and I certainly didn't feel like a woman.

"No, you are not too young. The younger you start sexual intercourse and the more partners you have, the greater your chance of developing this type of cancer. Last year we had a fifteen-year-old girl in the first stages of the disease."

"Oh."

By now the doctor had removed the duckbill thing he called a speculum and had put in his gloved hand and was feeling around. Knowing what to expect helped me to be a bit more calm and not to gasp as loudly as I had at the abortion clinic.

"I highly recommend you have an HIV test," he stated calmly as he poked and prodded.

"Dr. Womack, I don't think AIDS—"

Dr. Womack held up his hand to silence me. "Young lady, no one who has sex is immune to

AIDS. Especially those without a committed partner. I will order one for you."

I closed my mouth. No one believed me that Kyle couldn't have AIDS. No one accepted that was true . . . but me. I started to wonder if *I* was the one who was all wrong. *Oh, God,* I prayed as panic nudged me, *don't let that happen, too.*

Dr. Womack brought me out of my panicked thoughts. "Well, Julie, you are just about three months pregnant. I want you to dress and meet me in my office so I can give you some instructions."

Dr. Womack's office looked just like his personality. A plastic cube of pictures sat on his desk. It had various pictures of children, a woman, and himself. A rock with a painted face and felt feet sat next to the cube. A small sign in front of it faced me. It read, Beware of Pet Rock.

On the other side of the desk, perched upon a pedestal, was a brown globe with old, ancient-looking writing on it. I hadn't quite finished reading all the medical titles on his books when he came in.

The minute the door opened, he began talking.

"Julie, I'm so glad you came to see me so early in the pregnancy. Most girls your age don't want to admit they are pregnant until quite late in the pregnancy. This isn't safe for you or the baby. It is quite important for you to begin to eat properly and to take the vitamins I will prescribe for you.

The baby will benefit and so will you. You are still a youngster yourself. Your body is not quite ready to be producing babies; it still has not finished the job of growing and developing itself.

"Whenever you eat, I want you to remember you are feeding your baby the same thing. Cokes, Twinkies, candy bars are fine once in a while, but they don't give you or your baby the nutrition you both need to grow properly. You want your child to have a good chance in life and to be intelligent. Good nutrition on your part will help before your child is born.

"Eat three good meals a day or five to six snack-type meals. Some good snacks would be cheese, fruit, unsalted nuts, raw vegetables, or yogurt. Drink lots of liquids, like milk, juices, and water. Any questions?"

My head whirled from the amount of facts this doctor poured out in such a small amount of time. "No, I guess not."

"Next time before you come, write down any questions you have on a piece of paper. That way you won't forget any when you become flustered here in the office."

He wrote furiously on a couple of pieces of paper. "Here is your prescription for prenatal vitamins and a lab request slip."

He ripped both off their tablets and handed them to me. "Go to the lab at the hospital next door, and they will phone the results of the tests to me."

I looked at the lab slip with dismay. "I have two questions now," I said timidly.

"OK. Shoot."

"What does prenatal mean?"

"Before birth. Next?"

Holding up the lab slip, I asked, "Why do you need blood?"

"We do a set of five tests to check for syphilis, anemia, your blood type and factor, and to see if you are immune to German measles."

I nodded grimly, knowing my fate was sealed. The blood must come out.

"Julie, one more thing. I don't usually discuss finances with my patients, but you are a special case. Are your parents able to cover the cost of your prenatal care?"

"Well," I said hesitantly, "Mom and Dad's insurance will cover most of it."

"That's good. If there is ever any problem, let me know. We can then refer you to Medi-Cal for either cost sharing or total coverage.

"Also, I am going to recommend you to a Department of Health program. It's called Women, Infants and Children—WIC for short. There they will give you some coupons for food supplements that will help you to maintain the nutritional standards we spoke of earlier."

"I think Mom will appreciate that," I said with a chuckle. "I've been eating everything but the furniture, and she's been complaining about her enormous food bill."

Dr. Womack nodded as he listened, filling out a blue referral slip and then signing it.

"OK, Julie. We will see you in a month."

"Thanks, Dr. Womack."

12

MY second trip to Dr. Womack's office wasn't bad at all. Probably because this time I didn't have to take my clothes off.

They weighed me, took my urine sample, and checked my blood pressure and pulse. It felt strange to sit fully clothed on the exam table as I waited for Dr. Womack.

The minute he flew into the room, his mouth began to flap like his trailing coat. "Hi, Julie. Good to see you looking so well. I hope you are eating well, also. No salt or sugars, I hope. How about soft drinks? Not more than once in a while, please."

Meanwhile, he had me lift my dress to my belly button and lie down. He pulled out a round metal thing from his pocket.

"What are you going to do, build a house?" I asked, pointing to the measuring-tape canister.

"No, but you are building a baby, and I want to see how construction is going." He put one end of the measuring tape on the top of my pubic bone. The other end he held in place on my belly after he had poked around awhile. "This is part of your prenatal care routine. I will always measure your uterus to see how much it grows from one visit to the next."

Then he took a weird contraption that looked like a stethoscope a miner would have. He put a metal band around his forehead and the scope's plugs into his ears. He leaned over my belly and pushed down with his head, so the stiff amplifier was placed where my uterus ought to be.

"I don't hear any hammering yet," he announced with a smile. "Probably next time we will hear that baby tapping out messages with its heart. Sometime around the end of November, beginning of December, you ought to be able to feel the baby move.

"Any questions?"

"Only one," I said hesitantly.

"Only one?"

"Yeah. Is it OK to sleep on my stomach?"

"It's getting uncomfortable, isn't it?"

"Yes."

"It won't hurt the baby any. As time goes along it would be best for you to get used to sleeping on your left side."

"OK."

"See you in November. Remember to eat well! You want to build a good healthy baby."

"Right," I replied with no great conviction.

After I made my next appointment, I thought about how it was almost fun coming to the doctor's. I felt the people here understood me. They were the only ones I felt free to talk to about being pregnant.

I was embarrassed around Mom. I didn't know whether I should act like a daughter or a friend. I'd been avoiding Jan. I didn't want to give her the chance to say she didn't want me around anymore. I couldn't take added rejection. Especially from her.

And Stephanie? What a joke. She treated me like I was fragile or something. Most days now she was late to school. I was sure it was just so she didn't have to walk with me. I really didn't blame her. I felt as awkward as she did about it.

There wasn't much to talk about now. We couldn't talk about the boys she was dating because I felt funny and left out.

We couldn't talk about Baby because that brought up the subject of sex.

"So is it fun?" Stephanie asked hesitantly one day.

"Is what fun?" I said, confused.

"You know . . . being with a guy . . . like that."

She was worse than Mom. She couldn't say sex, either. "No, it wasn't fun," I snapped.

"Then why did you? . . ."

"I don't know. I hoped it would be just like ice cream."

"Just like ice cream?"

"You know, something great and wonderful."

She still looked awfully confused, and I could see the question again forming on her lips. "Ice cream?"

"Oh, forget it."

We walked the rest of the way to school in silence.

. . .

Mr. Silva was getting on my nerves. His incessant monotone was enough to drive anyone to the daydreaming ditch. At least I wasn't the only one who felt this way. It's amazing that he seemed totally oblivious to the passing of notes, chitchat, and hidden giggles.

Tom, the class clown, mimicked Mr. Silva, while David made his best paper airplanes.

No one understood why I didn't join their pranks anymore. Instead, I huddled in my coat, using the chill of December as an excuse to hide the changes going on in my body.

I was usually so far gone into a daydream that I didn't even notice what they did.

What was there to daydream about? *Baby*. Always Baby. Ever since I felt the flutter and tap of its first movements the fourth day of this month, Baby was heavy on my mind.

Even though Dr. Womack heard the heartbeat last visit, the baby didn't seem real until I actually felt it move. I still hadn't told anyone.

But now that I couldn't deny its existence, what was I going to do with it? I supposed I'd keep it. I wondered what it would look like?

Would I have to drop out of school? That might be kind of nice to avoid boring teachers like Mr. Silva. But what would I do with myself that would be less boring?

In PE I'd been wearing one of Matt's old sweatshirts. For once I'd found something useful about older brothers. I was sure he'd never miss it. The sweatshirt covered me all the way to the bottom of my shorts. It was so baggy, I'd bet I could wear it until the baby was born and no one would ever notice my growing figure.

I wasn't wearing any maternity clothes yet. I'd been wearing dresses every day. My friends thought I'd turned Little Miss Priss on them.

"Miss Marshall!"

From the tone of Mr. Silva's voice and all the faces turned toward me in rapt attention, I got the feeling it wasn't the first time my name had been mentioned.

"Miss Marshall, would you mind telling the class what is so important that you don't need to pay attention to the purpose of the judicial system?" His knuckles rapped the desk in thunderous rhythm.

I grabbed a strand of hair and pulled hard as I felt the red flow into my cheeks.

Mr. Silva keenly sensed I had no answer. His glare frightened me for the first time. "You will stay after class, Miss Marshall, and read about the judicial system during break time."

I nodded, grateful he wouldn't pry deeper.

"Heard you had a run-in with Mr. Silva," Stephanie said with laughter in her eyes as we met for lunch.

"Yeah, yeah," I said, hoping she would change the subject.

"My parents are going out tomorrow night and said I could have you over for pizza. Sound good?"

Poor Steph, still trying to be her old self. It all sounded so phony, but what better offer did I have? "Sure, I'd love to."

"Pizza's OK, isn't it?"

"Yes, Steph. Pizza's OK," I said a bit irritated.

. . .

My mouth watered as Stephanie opened the steaming box of pizza. Dr. Womack would probably have had a fit. All that salty meat. But who cares when your taste buds are so happy?

"I wonder if the baby will like pizza," I mused, patting the mound bulging under my dress.

"Are you going to keep it?" Steph's voice sounded dramatically shocked.

"I suppose. What else am I going to do with it?"

"I just figured you'd give it up for adoption."

"Adoption? Give up my own flesh and blood? How selfish can you get?"

"You think that's selfish?"

"Yes. Don't you?"

She shoved another bite into her mouth, chewing before answering. "No. I think it's a very loving thing to allow your child to grow up in a family."

I laughed. "What do you think this child will grow up in, a cage?"

I could tell she was getting frustrated. She kept shaking her hair till it almost got stuck in her pizza. "I mean a real family. Father, mother, maybe a sister or brother."

"My family is plenty. Besides, I happen to like babies. They're cute and fun to cuddle. And I'll have someone to love me."

"Julie, do you really think life will be so great with a baby?" Stephanie asked as she lifted the last piece of pizza from the box.

"No, I don't think it will be great. It will be life, and life has its ups and downs. A baby will help me cope. Give me some interest in life."

Stephanie shook her head hard, tossing her hair everywhere. "Babies don't help you cope; they help you to the loony farm."

"How do you know?" I snapped defensively.

She ignored the question and continued, "You

can't finish school, can't go to college. You have to work, but then some sitter is raising your child for you anyway. What kind of job do you think you can get without training?"

As I sat there watching her rant and rave, I twisted beautiful ringlets into my hair.

"Oh, sure, there is welfare. I can see it forming on your lips," Stephanie went on. "But welfare is the pits, the place no one can escape from. That's not life, that's barely existence."

"Oh, quit the lecture. You've always hated kids anyway."

"I have not. I just prefer to keep them out of my life until the future. I like friends my own age, and I want to keep that interest until I get married someday and have a baby of my own."

"Well, maybe that's why you're fuming. You're jealous because I beat you to it."

"Ha! I'm not jealous. You weren't listening. I said when I was married. You know, have a husband?"

"Who says I won't have a husband someday?" I stuck my bottom lip out.

"Do you think men are going to flock to a girl with a ready-made family? I've seen men flatter mothers by paying attention to their children. But when the moment of truth comes, they just can't accept some other man's kid."

My eyes were spitting fire. "So what makes you so wise and wonderful?"

Stephanie's focus dropped to the floor. "I've

been seeing Carol sometimes when she comes to visit her family."

"Carol? Since when did you become chummy with her?"

Steph flushed. "Since she started dating my brother."

"Oh," I said softly.

"Julie, it takes a very special man to marry someone with a child. My brother isn't even that type of guy."

"Well, what makes you think Kyle won't marry me?"

Her face turned to stone. She couldn't answer.

"Steph," I confided, "something deep inside tells me that soon Kyle will come and ask me to marry him. We'll have a small wedding and live a fun life with our baby in a cute apartment. I could take the baby on walks, pushing it all around in a stroller. We could go to the park. And when the baby gets old enough, I can push it on a swing or catch it at the bottom of a slide."

"And who gets up in the middle of the night with it?" Stephanie rudely interrupted.

I just stared at her.

"Don't you see, Julie? Those are just dandelion dreams."

"Dandelion dreams?"

"So beautiful, but very fragile. One puff and they're gone."

"Why can't it be that way?" I pleaded.

"Look at the reality, Julie. Kyle doesn't love you. I don't think he ever has."

The words stabbed my already aching heart. "What do you mean by that?" I asked hotly.

"Oh, Julie. I never wanted to tell you."

"Tell me what?" My heart sensed it and began to beat quickly.

"All summer, as you gazed into Kyle's eyes, his were wandering everywhere else."

"What proof do you have?" The tears began to flow.

"Julie, Kyle asked me out almost once a week all summer. Whenever you would be in the water, skiing, he would try to get cozy with me." Stephanie began crying as hard as I was.

"Why? Why didn't you tell me?"

"I didn't realize you two were . . . well . . . going to bed together. I thought it wouldn't harm you not to know if you two were just friends. After all, I knew Kyle would be leaving at the end of the summer."

I threw my arms around her for support as I sobbed. Oh, how I hated Kyle, but oh, how I wanted him to come love me like he used to. Or like I thought he used to. Now my life was ruined. How could I have been so blind and allowed myself to be used that way?

"Oh, Steph. Steph," I sobbed. "It *was* only a dream. A dandelion dream. The puff has come, and it's gone."

13

I woke up to the dancing drumbeats of rain on the roof. I peered through half-opened eyes at the waterfall steadily pouring from the eaves. Somehow the gloom was comforting.

A heaviness and ache had overtaken my heart for the last several days. Actually, I was surprised my heart could still beat with the weight attached to it. The ache made me breathe deeply and lower my head. Crying, ironically, did not come easily.

Whenever I finally did cry, the tears were from anger, and I would yell my lungs out as my pillow bounced off walls. The picture of Kyle and me, wet and happy on his dad's ski boat, had been ceremoniously burned.

I didn't care if I ever ate again. Food tasted lousy anyway. Especially ice cream or pizza.

Zombies walked with more direction than I did. I often didn't know where I was going and didn't really care. I could have walked in front of a truck and never even seen it. If Kyle didn't care, why should I?

He'd made me feel like day-old fish, a compost heap, or a dead cat—something that looks and smells so bad that everyone wants to hide it where they won't have to think about it anymore. So I hid myself to save them the trouble.

I rolled over in bed, struggling to get my emotions under control. How could he treat me like this? Why *shouldn't* he treat me like this? I wanted him to love me. I wanted to force him to love me. Didn't he promise to love me forever? How could he have used me and then dumped me like a piece of unwanted trash? I felt like an empty candy wrapper after all the sweetness has been eaten up.

At school, I didn't care who knew I was pregnant anymore. I'd even started to wear maternity clothes. I looked at my chair, sticking my tongue out at the pants draped there like a limp balloon.

Have you ever seen maternity pants? A square piece is cut out of the front where the zipper ought to be. In its place is stretchy fabric so your stomach can stick out as much as it wants. I hated those pants. They made me feel like a slob. I had to pull them up constantly. But what did I care? There was no one to look nice for anyway.

Just walking down the street could be a real

downer. People tried to be nice, but all they did was stare at my stomach as they talked. Some didn't even try to be nice. Their noses tipped into the air, or they pretended not to see me. They thought they were being so clever.

I heard all the rude jokes. Ten times over. The guys at school made certain I was within hearing distance before they began.

"Hey, look at her!"

"Yeah. Didn't you hear? Now that Julie Marshall can no longer be the star volleyball player, they've asked her to be the team's official ball carrier instead!"

Their shouts of laughter echoed down the hall, and I tried not to instinctively place a hand on my "ball" stomach.

At least the girls thought my pregnancy was neat. They gathered around me and wanted to touch and pat my stomach. But when it came to parties or other kinds of socializing, I wasn't invited.

With great effort, I managed to sit up in bed. Swinging my feet over the side, I tucked them into pink furry slippers. I shoved my arms into a tattered, moss-green terry robe and headed for the bathroom.

I was going to see Jan. She had been calling twice weekly for two months. I'd managed to avoid talking to her each time. But it was time to go see her and hear her rake me over the coals in person.

Rejection had become part of my daily diet. A little more wouldn't hurt.

Looking in the mirror, I saw a scowling prune face surrounded by wispy pieces of hair. I grabbed a comb and started yanking it through the snarls. Twenty minutes later, I was sloshing through puddles—I didn't see much point in trying to avoid them—on the way to Jan's cozy house on High Street. When I got there, my feet and stomach were soaked. Dad's old tan raincoat protected the rest of me.

Jan's green eyes beamed under raised brows when she saw me. "Julie! Come in! Come in!" I felt like a long-lost relative. She even hugged me, wet coat and all. So much for the rejection theory.

Jan hung my wet coat on an antique brass hook in her entryway.

I sank into her brown plaid sofa, realizing at once I had made a mistake. *I may never be able to get out of here without the help of a crane,* I thought to myself.

Stevie the cannonball shot out of the hallway and into my arms. Cuddling this squirming bundle that smothered me with kisses and hugs helped ease the gaping hole in my heart. Jan sat in a brown overstuffed chair, tucking her slipper-clad feet under her.

"How's your family?" Jan asked innocently.

"Oh," I said, gesturing with upturned palms and shrugged shoulders. "Fine, I guess."

"How are they taking your present situation?" she asked quietly.

"I could say the family is taking this whole pregnancy bit quite well." I let the bitterness start to flow. I didn't care that it had been two months since we last spoke. *She asked for it,* I reasoned. "I could say Tammy is a sweet sister who is sympathetic to my aches and pains. Or that she sticks up for me when her teasing, staring friends come around. I could say Matt has stopped playing basketball and eating long enough to admit that I exist. Or I could say Dad is loving and supportive."

I stopped picking at a loose thread in her couch and turned to watch water drip from my coat onto Jan's entry floor.

Jan remained silent, her face concerned.

"I could say all that, but it would be a lie." I twisted my hair furiously around my finger.

"So what's the truth?" Jan asked, leaning forward to pick up Stevie.

"Tammy pretends she doesn't know me in public, laughing and staring along with everyone else. Matt pretends he doesn't know me anywhere. He just lopes around with a sandwich in his left hand, while his right hand gently flutters up and down, dribbling an invisible ball."

Jan laughed quietly. "What can you expect from a twelve-year-old and a first-year college jock?"

I nodded slightly. "Dad looks right through

me, and I bet he would say some pretty mean things if he talked." I pondered what he would say, tightening the grip on my hair. "I guess for once I'm glad he isn't a talker."

"What do you want from them?" Jan asked gently as she stroked Stevie's hair.

"I want them to accept me. I always have." I paused to catch a stray tear. "I want them to love me in spite of this." I tapped my rock-hard stomach.

Jan nodded knowingly.

"What do *you* think I should do about this?" I tapped it again. "I've asked everyone else."

"What do they think?"

"Most of them say I should have gotten an abortion, but since I didn't, of course, I should keep it."

"Tookie! Tookie!" Stevie chimed in. Jumping from Jan's lap, he pointed a chubby finger toward the kitchen.

"Just a minute," Jan said to both of us. She left the room, returning with a pitcher of apple juice, some cups, and animal-shaped crackers. "Want some?"

"No, thanks."

"What does your mom say?" Jan held Stevie and helped him drink his juice.

"She says if I keep the baby, I will have to move out."

Jan's brow was poised for a question.

"She says it's not that she doesn't want me to

keep it. That's my decision. She feels I need to
have full responsibility for it. She can't be
counted on to be a live-in sitter."

"She's got a point."

"I guess. In off moments Tammy will tell me
how she hopes I'll keep it."

"What do you want to do?"

"Oh, I don't know. I'm so confused. I suppose
I should keep the baby, but I don't know if I can
handle the responsibility twenty-four hours a day.
I can hardly handle myself and my emotions
now."

"What emotions?" Jan asked softly.

"Mostly pain. Kyle hurt me so bad. That pain
and the uncertainty of the future never go away. I
dream about it, feel it kicking to remind me—" I
wiped at the tears as they escaped from my eyes.

Jan began to rock Stevie slightly. "The pain
will be there for a long time. It will lessen as the
years pass, and someday you will realize it's gone.
As for your uncertainty about the future, well . . .
all I can say is I truly believe it would disappear
into peace if you would give your problems over
to Jesus and trust him for the answer."

My mouth dropped open. "You mean he
would give me an answer? Straight from heaven?"

The beginnings of a smile touched the corners of Jan's mouth, and her green eyes danced. I
think she would have laughed if I hadn't been so
serious.

"It doesn't happen quite like that. His answers

come through reading his Word, the Bible, and spending lots of time in prayer about the problem."

"So how do you know when you have the answer?"

"Peace. God never lets me rest until I've made the right decision. The decision still may be hard or painful. But when I follow through, I have a peace of mind and heart that I have done the best thing."

"So what do you think I should do?" I asked again. I hoped she might have an answer from God for me.

"I can't make that decision for you."

"Thanks a heap."

Jan shook a friendly finger at me. "Hear me out. I have a friend living in the city who does counseling with pregnant teenagers. Maybe you should go talk to her."

So I did. Roberta worked for the Children's Placement Society. They are an adoption agency. But Roberta surprised me. She didn't push adoption.

I went to see Roberta several times. We sat in her office at the Society, a renovated Victorian house. Her window looked out over the street that dropped steeply away from us, eventually finding its end near the Bay.

She always gave me a paper clip before we began to talk. She would take one, too, and we would both proceed to destroy them during each hour or two we had together.

She always wore something in a color I would never give a second glance at in a store. Bright purple or burgundy were her favorites. But she looked fabulous. The colors set off the silver in her hair. She looked like she had to be at least fifty, but when she spoke, I knew she understood me.

We talked a lot about the hassles of being pregnant, about family and friends. Sometimes we even cried about Kyle. Roberta was fun and frustrating to talk to. Fun because I could tell her anything, frustrating because she made me think about this whole thing—something I'd rather not have done.

Sometimes I felt as though I was in school. I mean, she gave me homework at the end of each visit. I must confess it was the most challenging and interesting homework I've ever had to do. Besides, I never got a grade and never had to turn it in. We simply talked about the results.

First, I had to shop for prices on everything Baby would need for its first year. Clothes, diapers, food, formula, and all that kind of stuff. Then she had me break the cost down into weeks and months. Next, I had to look at housing rentals, food and clothing costs for me, then add it all up and see how the budget would work under welfare allotments or under minimum wages for a month.

I couldn't believe how much baby stuff cost.

One lousy can of formula was almost four dollars! She said you needed a couple of cans a day at first and about one later on.

Food was close to forty cents a jar. One crib sheet was twelve dollars, T-shirts were five dollars. Outfits were outrageous at fifteen to twenty-five dollars!

Added up all for a whole year, well, the total made me shudder. A tight squeeze is a freeway in comparison.

Roberta also had me write a little essay on, What is a parent? That was hard. I never thought of me being a parent. Not like Mom and Dad. They are parents. I'm a kid.

The last thing she had me do was make two lists. At the top of one sheet of paper I wrote "pros." That was where I'd write the benefits. I drew a line down the middle and labeled one side "adoption," the other "parenting." Then I wrote "cons" at the top of a second piece of paper, for the negatives. Like with the first sheet, I wrote "adoption" on one side and "parenting" on the other. Now I was ready.

For the next two weeks, I thought a lot about the subject. Anytime I thought of something good or bad about being a mother, I wrote it on the appropriate piece of paper. I did the same thing with adoption.

Roberta said that this would help me to make up my mind. Not really. It almost made things more difficult. Now I didn't want to do either.

14

FOG hugged the city so tightly I felt I almost couldn't breathe. It even seemed to seep through the cracks around the windows.

I looked at Roberta and straightened my paper clip in one angry jerk.

"I don't think it's possible to love the baby and give it up for adoption," I said rudely.

Roberta raised one eyebrow, so characteristic of her when she begins to listen intently. "Why not?"

"Don't you understand?" I exclaimed hotly. "The baby is my own flesh and blood! Give it to strangers? I can't do that!"

In her forever even-tempered voice, Roberta replied, "Hopefully, no girl ever has to give her child to strangers. It's her choice for them to remain anonymous. Intimate details of several adoptive families can be given to the mother so she can make her own choice as to where her child will belong."

I tapped my finger on the arm of the chair. I was still angry, but she had aroused my curiosity. "What do you tell someone about the families?"

"Everything but the names. You can know their ages, hobbies, likes, dislikes, schooling, what they do for a living, even their physical characteristics. Most important, we tell the mother how the parents feel a child should be raised."

"Do you think these people could love an adopted child as though it were their own?" I asked doubtfully.

"Yes." Roberta laughed softly. "Some have forgotten the child is adopted. Adoption is the biggest gift of love a person can make."

"How can it be a gift of love?" I asked, my anger welling up inside again. I tapped the paper clip on her desk. "I think it's plain and simple selfishness. I might as well wear a banner proclaiming, 'This baby is an obstacle to my plans, so I'm getting rid of it.'" I looked at her triumphantly.

"First of all, look at your baby's future," Roberta pointed out. "What kind of life do you want the child to have? What kind of love, shelter, clothing, food, and so on?" She paused a moment waiting for me to answer. I stared at her, bouncing my foot. "And what about you?" she reasoned. "Do you want to continue with school? get married? What do you want your future to hold?"

Her voice, always gentle, never accusing, bore holes in my ideas.

I began to realize I was being selfish by never thinking of what the baby's future might hold with just me, an uneducated teenager, as a mother. No father. I looked down at the scarlet carpet, drawing designs with the toe of my tennis shoe.

"So you don't think a girl should keep her baby?" I accused softly.

"If you are able to meet your child's needs to your satisfaction while not neglecting your own needs, then you should keep the baby." She set down her paper clip, folding her hands on the desk. "But if your needs are not being met, your child's needs won't be either." She paused a moment, then continued, "This is why adoption can be a gift of love. It can be a gift of love to yourself. You need to develop your own interests and life before you will be able to pour all you have into a child. For the child, it's a gift of love because you are making certain it will receive the physical, emotional, and material support it needs. And . . . it's a gift of love to the adoptive parents. Most have tried unsuccessfully for many years to have their own children. Think of what it could mean to them."

"I guess all that makes sense," I relented. "But I'm sure adoption is not for me."

Roberta smiled. "Whatever your decision is, I will stand behind you and support you. But I remind you that it must be *your* decision. You are the one who must live the rest of your life with that decision."

As I drove home from our final visit, I thought about what she had said. I could hardly help it. Her final words stuck to me like a peanut-butter sandwich that glues itself to the roof of your mouth.

At the same time, I was tired of thinking. I felt like my brain was all wrinkled up like a used tissue. I tried to shift my attention to the road that curved and wound endlessly. It was good to be out of the fog of San Francisco and to see the hills part and roll away from the road. Grapevines, cut back for the winter, had once looked like thousands of little marching men. Now they looked like a bunch of dead sticks.

I felt like a dead stick. The ache in my heart was the only thing that assured me that I was quite alive. The hole that had to be there was yawning as though it would swallow me in a very short time.

I had to call Kyle. Maybe he felt the emptiness inside, too.

Each town I passed was still decorated for Christmas. The decorations reminded me of that awful, strained day. I was so glad *that* was over. It was just such a wonderful feeling to know you'd ruined everyone's Christmas!

For one thing, I could tell that no one knew what to buy a pregnant girl who hadn't made a decision about her baby. I got a lot of socks and a diary. Wonderful. It had been a total bust.

When I reached home, depression hung over me like a thundercloud. I helped Mom clean a bit, then sneaked up to my room.

The telephone receiver shook in my hand. "Hello, Mrs. Browning? Is Kyle there?"

She paused a moment, probably trying to place the voice. "Oh, honey," she said in her refined manner, as though she knew perfectly well who I was. "Kyle and that cute little girl, oh, what's her name? . . . oh yes, Barb, have gone out this evening. Too bad it's so chilly and foggy."

"Thank you, Mrs. Browning." I hung up the phone very carefully.

My pillow hit the wall in record time, and I refused to join the family for Saturday night television.

As I crawled into bed, I glanced at my barren calendar. My birthday was in a week and a half. I hoped everyone would forget. I didn't need any more socks.

• • •

The fire warmed my hands and face. I had been spending much of my time at Jan's house. It was the only place I felt completely accepted and peaceful. The smell of rising bread dough made me feel like I had crawled into a warm and safe blanket.

Jan and I sipped tea from pottery mugs, helping the fire ward off the chill filtering into our bones.

Jan was sitting on the floor, singing a silly song to Stevie as she changed his diaper. My thoughts began to drift again. What Roberta said had been going over and over in my mind like a skipping record. Maybe I'd been wrong about adoption. Maybe I shouldn't have been so quick to condemn others for doing it just because it was something I couldn't do.

I rubbed my stomach where the baby kicked mercilessly.

"Where's your mind gone, Julie?"

I looked up from my reverie, shrugging my shoulders. Jan looked at me intently. I hadn't noticed she had quit singing. "You seem concerned about something."

I sipped some tea. "I guess I am. The problem of adoption is still making me crazy . . . right, wrong, selfish, loving." I shook my head. "I just don't know."

Jan had to take a diaper pin from her mouth before she could speak. "The authority I rely on most speaks quite highly of adoption."

I perked up. "Really? What authority? What does it say?"

"God is my authority and he—"

"I should have known," I interrupted, shaking my head. I looked at her mockingly. "Who did he ever adopt?"

"Me."

If Jan's eyes hadn't been looking directly into mine and her face radiant, I would have thought she was joking. So my voice was laced with only a soft sarcasm. "You are kidding, right?"

"I'm not kidding. He adopted me five years ago when I lived in Los Angeles." She kissed Stevie's cheek and sent him playing with his cars.

"So how does *God* go about adopting people?"

Jan smiled softly. "The process is similar to our adoptions. For example, a couple takes the first step when they want to seek a child. They pay a legal fee, papers are signed, and the child is given to the new parents for them to feed, clothe, and care for as though it were their own."

I began to laugh. "So God went to an adoption agency, I suppose?"

Jan tipped her head back and laughed. "Hardly," she said and then sipped some more tea. "That is where the difference comes in. God paid the price and has the seal all ready. But the children must come to him for that legal seal. He won't force anyone to be his child who doesn't want to be."

"Why would anyone want to be his child?" I asked skeptically.

Jan didn't hesitate. "The benefits are so great. I

feel sorry for those who prefer what little they have to what they could have as a child of God."

"What benefits?" I asked with rising curiosity.

Jan smiled. "Mostly he gives new inner qualities: patience, gentleness, peace, kindness. He cares for our physical needs, too. There are all kinds of benefits a perfect father can bring."

"Perfect?" I felt myself sinking into a bog of hopelessness. "Oh, Jan, he wouldn't want to adopt me."

"Why not?" Jan gently demanded.

"Isn't this reason enough?" I tapped my stomach. "I would be out of place as the child of a perfect father. And this is just my most obvious mistake, to say nothing of all the rest. I'm not good enough to be his adopted child."

Jan's expression softened. "No one is good enough to be a child of God. But he was willing to pay the high price for our mistakes so adoption would be possible."

I moved to sit on the braided rug with her. "But what difference will it make for *me?*"

"A difference in everything. In your whole life." Jan's face displayed confidence. "I now have meaning to my life. God gives me direction, constant help, and guidance. He gives me strength in weakness and peace during storms." She ignored Stevie, who ran cars over her arms and legs.

I watched him a moment, then asked quietly, "How does someone get adopted?"

"It says in the Bible that Jesus, God's Son, is

the way. We can't approach God on our own because God is perfect. Jesus is the required legal fee. His death was the price the Father paid to make us new persons who can be at home in his family."

I tried to grasp all these things and put them in an order I understood. I sifted and filed until words and phrases made sense. Like learning a new language. . . .

Jan's eyes took on a new glow. "Then comes the best part. He sends a part of himself to live inside you. Kind of like the seal put on adoption papers to make it legal. The seal is God's own Spirit, and he will never leave you. The seal cannot be altered."

I could feel the baby turning another somersault. I tried to calm the flutter in my heart.

"Jan." My voice broke. "I want to be one of God's adopted children." For once in my life, I had made a major decision. And there was no doubt—it was the right one.

"OK, why don't you tell him that?"

"Tell him? Do you mean *pray?* I don't know how to pray."

Jan cocked her head. "How do you talk to me?"

I shrugged my shoulders. "I don't know. I just do."

"That's how you talk to God," Jan said simply. "Just like you would talk to me."

I picked at a string from the rug. I opened my

mouth and drew in a deep breath. I squeezed my eyes shut. "God," I said hesitantly, "I don't quite know what to say." I opened my eyes and looked at Jan. She smiled encouragingly, and I went on. "I want you to take over this mess I call my life. I want you to adopt me, change me, help me. Forgive me for all the dumb and wrong stuff I've done, and I want that life you promised, too, OK?"

Jan reached over and touched my hand. "Thank you, Father, for my friend Julie. I'm so glad you answered my prayers for her—that she would find you. Thanks."

I opened my eyes and looked around. Everything looked the same. I could still see and hear Stevie *vrrooom!*-ing his cars around the house. I could still smell the bread. Yet something was missing. I looked down and blurted out, "It's gone!"

Jan's face furrowed with confusion. "What's gone?"

"The hole in my heart. It's finally gone." I looked at Jan, my mouth twisted into a cockeyed little smile.

Leaning over, she gave me a hug.

The phone rang, rudely disrupting our quiet joy. "Julie, it's your mom," Jan said.

I awkwardly got up from the floor, taking the receiver from her. "Hi, Mom."

Her voice was strained. "I just thought you might like to know. Kyle's here."

15

THE rain had stopped. Even the coldest January bore little or no snow to our town.

I put my hands in my pockets in a vain attempt to keep them warm. I tucked my head down, looking at the ground as I walked. This time I carefully avoided the numerous puddles, little gray mirrors flecked with bits of leaves.

I didn't want to think about home. I didn't want to think about Kyle. Yet not to think about them was an impossibility.

Why did he come? I shuddered with fear, cold, and anticipation. Perhaps my knight had come to bear me away on his white horse.

Oh, why hadn't I worn the orchid-pink maternity top I'd splurged five nights' baby-sitting earnings on? Instead, I had worn my tattered blue thing with a grease spot in the middle of the left pocket. Tacky at best.

I slipped around to the back of the house and stepped out of my wet and muddy shoes. Countless occasions of sneaking in the house late at night had made me a pro at turning the back doorknob silently. I knew the spots in the floor that creaked and carefully sidestepped them on the way to the living room.

If Kyle didn't hear my approach, he was sure to hear the pounding of my heart. I wanted to get a good solid look at him before I had to speak. I wanted to see if memory had distorted reality.

I stopped under the stucco arch. My memory had done no justice to what I saw.

Kyle was stunning in his sapphire blue and tan rugby shirt. Blue was his best color, and he looked warm and huggable.

Kyle was talking to my mom, his hands moving in vivid description of his latest escapades. Without even seeing them, I knew his eyes sparkled with self-confidence. It struck me as strange that he could still look Mom in the eye after all that had happened.

He was so poised, so arrogant, and so better-looking than anyone I had ever seen. I wanted to run and throw my arms around him. At the same time, I wanted to grab the telephone from the table next to me and throw it at him.

Mom must have seen me from the corner of

her eye. She turned her head and smiled at me. Kyle followed her gaze and turned to voice an elegant hello. I watched all pretense come crashing down around him as he stared at me. Or rather, at my stomach.

Mom quietly slipped from the room as he tried to speak.

I felt bad about my enjoyment in watching him flounder. I never would have believed Kyle knew what it meant to be nervous. Yet there he was, his tongue stammering wildly. "I never . . . uh . . . never . . ."

His eyes continued to stare about two stories below my chin. This new voice was so unlike the confident smoothness I had grown used to. He tried again, his hand waving around like a confused bird. "I didn't expect you to look like . . . uh . . . this."

I wanted to ask, "What did you expect a pregnant girl to look like?" Instead, I carefully dressed my voice with courtesy. "How are you?" I asked.

He again tried to look me in the eye, but there seemed to be a magnet pulling his eyes down to stare at my very round figure.

"Uh, fine. I guess." He looked awkwardly around the room. "My mom made me come," he blurted.

If I had hackles, they would have risen in a flash. Instead, I threw my words at him like stones. "Well, *fine*. You've done your duty. If you don't have anything else to say, why don't you leave." I gritted my teeth into a rude smile. I didn't want to lose my battle with the tears beginning to form in my eyes.

I really didn't want him to leave, but his gorgeous, untouched presence suddenly made me acutely aware of my lumpy ugliness.

Bewildered, he turned to leave. Halfway to the door, he stopped in his tracks. Reversing, he extended a shaking hand with a wrapped package. "Kind of a combination birthday and Christmas gift," he said softly.

"Thanks," I muttered. *I bet his mom chose it, bought it, and wrapped it. Another duty,* I thought angrily.

He left without waiting for me to open the gift.

As best I could, I ran up the stairs to my room. I wanted to punch the baby for making me unable to throw myself onto the bed. Instead, I sat on a chair and sobbed.

I let the tears drop onto the pretty paper box. Golden yellow roses decorated the top. I wiped under my eyes and slowly pulled off the yellow satin ribbon. Removing the lid, I carefully pulled back the rustling white tissue paper.

The pretty box with navy blue kneesocks inside went crashing against the wall. As I watched them fall crumpled to the floor, I shouted through fresh tears, "I hate you, Kyle Browning! I hate you!"

. . .

Birthday. Over. I only received two gifts worth mentioning. The first and best was an easy-to-read-and-understand Bible. The second was a notebook. Both were from Jan.

I started getting up every day fifteen minutes early to read a paragraph or two from the book of John. Then I wrote what I thought about it in my little notebook. Mostly I wrote questions.

Jan had agreed to read the same thing, and then we talked about what we'd found. It was fascinating.

I never knew the Bible could actually relate to my life, but I was actually learning! The people in the Bible were real; they just lived in a time and place I wasn't used to yet.

Anyway, the book of John was about the life of Jesus, and boy was I learning about how he wanted me to live! Anytime I yelled at Tammy for intruding on my privacy or whatever, I didn't feel satisfied anymore. I felt guilty. I kept getting gentle reminders to do better, but change isn't very easy.

I had to admit it, though, it seemed Tammy was getting easier to live with. She didn't go out of her way to irritate me like she used to. She even came to me and put her hand on the baby to wait until it moved. She always got the biggest kick out of that. I think loving the baby was her way of also loving me.

Even Matt was becoming civilized. He had actually gone out of his way a few times to say hello and a halfhearted "How are you?" For him that was progress.

Jan said they were reacting to the change in me. I wasn't so sure. I didn't feel changed.

The best thing that had happened, though, involved Dad. He came in from work one night all grubby. He walked over to where I sat in the overstuffed chair and pulled me out of it. I was a little scared until I looked into his eyes.

Dad had always had the most expressive eyes. After all these months of disappointment flooding his eyes, the expression I saw there had now changed to kindness.

His rough hands clasped my arms gently. His lips moved as if he were going to speak. I thought I saw a tear come to one eye, but he gave me no chance to make sure. He pulled me close and hugged me.

My nose tickled with wood dust as he stroked my hair once. He spoke quietly in his brief way. "Hi, Jule."

He let go and took the stairs three at a time. It wasn't long before I heard the shower running.

I smiled. That was Dad's special way of accepting me and my situation.

Not that my world had turned rosy. Or maybe it had—but roses have thorns, you know. And I had two big ones.

The first was Stephanie. As close as she and I

had always been, something was splitting us apart. I tried to blame it on differing interests and figured that everything would be fine after the baby was born. As it was, we could talk about all sorts of things, but again, she couldn't socialize much more than that with me. She was too wrapped up in the guy of the week. So when we were together, she'd toss her hair and tell me about her latest fling with who knows who. Whoever he was, she was in love with him. Two weeks later that guy was a creep, and someone new had taken his place.

We still had our cinnamon rolls at break time together, and we continued to eat lunch and watch the world go by. But it just wasn't the same.

I tried one day to tell Stephanie what had happened to me since I'd asked Jesus to change my life. She laughed, then sobered, admitting, "You have changed, Julie. You aren't depressing to be around anymore. It's like you have something to look forward to." Then she pouted. "It's also as if you have a special secret you can't pass on. You don't need me anymore."

"That's not true, Steph." I put down my half-eaten sandwich. "The secret is easy to pass on."

Steph waved her hand at me. "I don't need your secret. I'm doing fine on my own." She sipped her Coke slowly. "All I really want is to be needed. . . ." She let her voice drift off dramatically. I figured her new acting class was to be thanked for that.

"I will always need your friendship, Stephanie," I affirmed. I said it, and I knew it was true, but I suspected I wouldn't always have her friendship.

The gulf was growing too wide for either of us to bridge the gap. Slowly we were rising to the level of social friends instead of intimate, "tell-all" friends. Unless our worlds could find a spot of common ground, I was afraid all intimacy would soon be lost.

Thorn number two: what to do with the baby.

Mom was great about poking me with this one. For example, I had a terrible case of heartburn Valentine's night when Mom thought it would be a wonderful time to discuss the future. She let herself into my room without knocking. "Have you decided what you are going to do about the baby yet?" she asked.

My pen dropped on the desk with a clatter. "No. I don't want to talk about it now, either." Deliberately, I picked up the fallen pen and returned my attention to my English paper.

Mom smoothed her apron carefully over her lap. I could see her plotting her next move in this little game of battle baby we had going.

"Don't you think," she said with a forced smile, "the time is coming when you need to finalize what you are going to do?"

Impatiently, I tilted my head. "Yes, Mother."

She'd obviously blown that move. She sighed. "Well, let me know if I can help."

Smiling a sickening sweet smile, I nodded. "Of course."

Finally, she left and I could wallow in misery and heartburn. A bath sounded comforting. As I slipped into the hot water, frosted with bubbles, I thought about my options.

No matter which way I turned, I got poked with another thorn.

One day I would see a mother with her cute little one all bundled up, its little pink face so serene and sweet as it slept—and I'd want more than anything to keep my baby. I wanted to hold it, take it to the park, and push it in the swing.

Then I'd spend time with Stevie and Jan. That's when I saw the responsibility and the hours of time involved in training a child. Or I'd listen to all the plans of the kids at school. They'd discuss colleges, careers, and dreams, and it all sounded so exciting. If I kept the baby, it would be hard to do all that. Maybe any of it.

That's when I'd start thinking maybe adoption was the best thing for me. But never to see my child again? How could I do that?

If only I could see my life one, two, three years ahead. If only I could see twenty years down the road. If only . . . Thoughts like that kept running around and around in my head, making me dizzy with frustration.

This whole thing was a relentless nightmare.

Most nights I just let my tears flow down my face. "Oh, God," I prayed softly. "What am I going to do? Why aren't there more choices? Why? Why? Why?"

• • •

March winds were blowing their cold air mercilessly through my clothes as though they were an open window. The clouds hung heavy and low. It would only be a matter of time before their bellies burst forth again with cold, gray rain.

My emotions were as unpredictable as the wind. Dr. Womack told me that was normal, along with a host of other problems: leaking breasts, my constant heartburn, stomach itching, the brown line on my stomach, stretch marks (ugh!), and even the twenty pounds I'd gained.

I wouldn't call twenty pounds normal. I'd call it *fat*.

One afternoon I forced my heavily loaded body up the stairs to Dr. Womack's office, cringed properly when the nurses weighed me, and waited to ask a very important question.

"How is everything?" Dr. Womack asked, bending over the lump on the table (me), listening to the baby's heartbeat.

"Fine, I guess."

He peered at me over the top of his glasses. "You don't sound convinced."

I shifted my weight and sat up awkwardly. "I am getting quite tired of this little bundle."

He patted my hand. "You don't have much longer to go. I still suspect your due date of April 18 is a good guess."

I let my face fall. "You mean you can't tell for sure?"

He laughed. "If I could do that, I'd be a rich man. Next visit we will do an internal exam."

I wrinkled my face in disgust, twisting my hair around my finger.

Dr. Womack went on. "We will check to see if your cervix has begun to thin out or dilate. This will give us a better idea when the baby might come."

"Dr. Womack," I said, changing the subject, "I have an important question. Why do I have to go to school?"

"You don't *have* to go to school. It is best for you to remain active. School helps with that and with the pregnant boredoms." He paused, ripples traveling up from his brows to the middle of his balding head. "I also presume you want to graduate next year?"

I nodded sheepishly. Baby or no baby, I wanted to graduate. As usual he was right. The benefits of continuing in school did outweigh the problems. At least the jokes about me had finally stopped. The kids were getting used to me and talking to me more.

It seemed, though, that everywhere I went, I felt all eyes focusing on my stomach. But you know what the absolute worst part was about school? Sitting in those uncomfortable hard desks.

I looked up at Dr. Womack and said a half-hearted "Thanks."

He smiled. "See you in two weeks."

16

3:22 A.M.

I wished the moon could talk. His face looked so wise. His lips were pursed and ready to speak. He was golden as he peeked over the hills, then changed to a frosty white as he climbed higher into the sky to watch over the proceedings below.

I felt as though it was just he and I awake. I couldn't sleep with that nagging pain in my lower back.

I never expected contractions to be like this. An incredible tightness that pushed downward had overtaken my body. It all took place inside, my outside skin wasn't even involved.

During each contraction, I could feel the entire outline of my uterus.

The pain in my back came at the same time as

the contractions in the front. Both pains together made me real uncomfortable. Walking around made me feel much better. I guess it gave me a false sense of accomplishing something.

If I could have sat still long enough, I'd have written in my diary. I knew exactly what I'd have said:

> April 24. My body has begun to churn and creak and groan. I am going to have a baby, and it will probably be today. Will I be able to make a wise decision about its future? The baby has been with me so long. I know its every move. We are a part of each other. It can't leave me now.

When I last spoke with Roberta ten days ago, she seemed matter-of-fact when I told her I was unable to make a decision. She told me I needn't decide anything final until after the baby was born. I did choose a family, though. Just in case. They loved the outdoors, pets, children, and had an excellent education. He was an engineer, and she was a teacher. Best of all, both had Jesus as a friend, just like I did.

I caught my breath as another contraction began tightening its grip on me. I realized I'd been denying the baby's existence even until that day. Then the truth overwhelmed me. Involuntarily, I shivered.

I was very, very scared.

6:00 A.M.

The contractions were so hard that I had to stop and either sit down or bend over when one hit. It was impossible to walk during a contraction. I expected Mom to be up any minute to get ready for work. I hated to intrude in her life with my business. Why couldn't I have had the baby on a weekend so it would be more convenient for everyone?

10:00 A.M.

The hospital walls were white and bare except for a huge black-and-white clock. I got to stare at it while I sat in bed. I could watch the second hand slow down during each contraction.

The nurse had shown me how to breathe deeply during a contraction. It helped me relax a bit, and the pain wasn't so severe.

Mom patiently sat beside me. She stared blankly at the television, jumping to life only when I began to moan with another contraction.

It was going to be a long day. Dr. Womack had already come in to check me. He predicted the baby would come sometime in the evening.

I was dilated three centimeters. That meant, he said, the opening in the uterus, where the baby must come out, had opened to about three fingers' width. It had to open to ten centimeters before the baby could fit through.

11:00 A.M.

A plump nurse with a lavender uniform walked

in carrying a small tray. "Hi," she said sweetly. "I'm going to prep you now."

I looked to my mother quickly, then back to the nurse. "What do you have to do?"

She filled a small bowl with warm water from the sink, looking over her shoulder as she spoke. "It isn't painful. We shave a small area of your pubic hair. Just around the vaginal opening. Then we give you a small enema."

I flinched, scrunching my face at the word *enema*. The word alone sounded hideous.

The nurse noticed my intense displeasure and held up a small plastic bottle with a long plastic tip on the end. "See this?"

I nodded.

"We use less than half of this."

I stared and grabbed the bedrails as another pain hit. She waited until the contraction was over before continuing.

"Lie on your side, and we'll get to work." She talked about her children as she shaved me. She was right. I think she made about six strokes with the razor, then was done. I gasped as the fluid filled my rectum from the enema bottle.

She spoke quickly. "I will help you out of bed and to the toilet. Sit there, and try to hold the fluid in as long as possible. The cleaner you are, the more comfortable you will be when it comes time to push."

I lowered myself onto the toilet, using the

handrails on each side. Thankfully, she closed the door, allowing me some dignity.

I was OK until a contraction came. My moaning brought both my mother and the nurse running. They opened the door, and I motioned them away.

Five minutes later I came out, bent like an old lady checking out her garden.

12:00 noon
They offered to bring Mom some lunch. I readily agreed. I was starving. But I didn't get anything except ice chips. The nurse said I shouldn't eat. It might make me vomit later when the contractions got harder.

Harder? I thought they were hard enough already.

I was now dilated to five centimeters. Halfway there.

2:00 P.M.
I detested not being in control of myself. But now I was at the mercy of another force.

The contractions were like ocean waves. The power would build and build to a peak. Suddenly it would subside, losing strength until all was relaxed.

A few minutes would pass, then another wave. Each contraction was stronger than the last. With each one I gripped the handrails, trying not to cry out.

I looked pleadingly into my mother's eyes,

imploring for her to help. Her eyes returned a look of understanding, of love, of remembrance.

The nurse came in through the haze of pain, offering a shot of Demerol to ease the force. I turned her down, not wanting to lose the remaining control I had left.

The next contraction brought about a release of pressure and an abundance of wet warmth.

"Mom, get the nurse, quick."

Without hesitating, Mom ran and brought back a nurse.

"What's happening?" I pleaded.

The nurse took one look at the large blue pad protecting the bed and smiled. "Your water broke."

"My what?"

"The water sac that surrounds the baby has ruptured. Your contractions should go a little faster and harder now."

She quickly changed the pad to a dry one and bustled out the door.

3:00 P.M.
The nurses on the new shift came in one at a time to check on me. One offered Demerol. I agreed this time.

I was now dilated to seven centimeters. I almost didn't care.

4:30 P.M.
The way Mom stared at me gave me the creeps. I wished she'd leave.

Dr. Womack came to check on me again. He was smart to avoid dumb questions like How are you? or How's it going? He didn't stay long. Just long enough to tell me I was in transition. Whatever that meant.

I was tired of all this. I wanted to go home and maybe come back to finish this later . . . then again, maybe not.

Mom left to get a Coke. I hoped she would hurry back.

6:00 P.M.

I was sitting on the toilet, holding onto the rails beside it as though they were the only things keeping me from falling in.

My body uncontrollably folded in half, bearing down as though I had to expel something.

The nurse pounded on the door. "Are you OK, Julie?"

I could barely talk. "Yeah. I feel like I'm constipated. That's all."

"Come out. *Now.*" Her voice sounded urgent. "That feeling is the baby coming down the birth canal."

I pulled myself up using the rails. I couldn't have gotten up without them. The nurse opened the door and helped me to bed.

"Lie back and relax," she said gently. "I'm going to do a manual exam to check you again."

I groaned slightly but obeyed. I didn't feel like arguing.

Her gentle hands probed as she spoke. "Yes, the baby's head is beginning to protrude through the cervical opening. Next time you have a contraction, I want you to push with all your might."

She showed me how to pull myself up by my knees and bear down as hard as I could, holding my breath.

7:05 P.M.

Two nurses entered the room. Both were dressed in blue scrub clothes.

One positioned herself at the head of my bed, the other at the foot. The one at the foot of the bed spoke firmly. "OK, Julie. The baby's head is crowning. I can see it right at the entrance to your vagina. It is time to go to Delivery."

She and the other nurse pushed the bed through the doorway and down the hall. Under normal circumstances, I would have been embarrassed at even this short jaunt, considering I was wearing practically nothing. At that moment, though, I couldn't have cared less.

They wheeled me into a brightly lit room. All around were contraptions with cords and tubes hanging on them. In the corner was a small bed. Clear plastic sides revealed a tiny mattress and sheets.

In the center of the room was the delivery table. It looked almost identical to the doctor's exam table, only larger.

The nurses helped me to get onto it. It wasn't

an easy task. Because of the baby in the birth canal, I couldn't bend.

I had the distinct feeling the baby would come out at any moment, but they didn't seem to be the least bit worried.

Dr. Womack appeared, eyes crinkled in a smile. A mask covered the rest of his jolly face. "Hello again, Julie. Let's get to work so we can see this baby!"

I just looked at him, panting with fright and pain. My head felt light and heavy at the same time.

Dr. Womack patted my leg. "It's OK, Julie. You are doing just fine."

A mirror, placed just beyond my left foot, reflected a distorted image of my lower body. I could see the baby's head forcing its way out.

Dr. Womack gave me an injection right next to the baby's head. "This will numb you so I can make a small incision. The size of the baby's head indicates your skin might tear if we don't."

I felt much stretching, pressure, and a strong movement as the baby's head came out with the next contraction.

"Just one more push," Dr. Womack encouraged, "and we'll have the rest of the baby out, too."

It took three pushes and the baby came sliding out. I panted and cried with relief. I tried to peer down at the little, slimy, pink-and-purple thing covered with white cornstarch they claimed to be my baby.

A small cry filled the room as it sucked in its first breath of air. I looked at my baby in wonder. "It's a boy."

My whole mind could have been blown away with a feather. How could that living being have come from inside me? I wanted to touch it, to hold it.

The nurse wrapped him up in a warm towel and laid him in my arms. I suddenly felt timid and awkward holding this little warm bundle of baby. I thought about Roberta and the family hoping and waiting for him. Yet . . . how could *I* give away this little wonder?

"Nurse," I said cautiously, "can you take him?" I felt badly that I didn't want to hold him anymore, but fatigue and fear came over me, and I was afraid I might drop him. I looked into the nurse's eyes. "Can someone go tell Mom?"

She nodded. "Someone already has."

I felt the doctor pushing on my suddenly flat, Jell-O-like stomach. "The placenta will be out in a moment," he announced.

I hadn't thought of that. After nourishing the baby for nine months, its job was done. It came out purple, red, blue, and white—a many-colored jellyfish.

Dr. Womack sewed up the incision he had made to allow for the baby's head. When he finished, he took off his gloves and clasped my hand tightly between his two strong ones. "You done good, Julie." He winked and gave my hand a final squeeze before he sailed out the door.

The transfer back to my rolling bed was a breeze. A quiet nurse wheeled me to a private room. I was grateful to whoever had the sensitivity to my situation. I needed to be alone.

Aside from being so tired I could sleep a week, I thought I might starve. Finally I was brought a tray of delicious food, but when I began to eat, my appetite fled.

Mom came in to smile and stare. I stopped my picky eating and declared, with my fork waving for emphasis, "I don't want any visitors except Jan."

Mom looked disappointed. "Not even Dad or Stephanie?"

"No, Mom. No one." I turned my head away as my eyes filled with tears. "I have too much to think about." Besides, I didn't want the world to prance through to stare at me, the sideshow freak.

When morning came, I begged to see my little boy again. My son. I couldn't believe what had happened the day before until I had touched him again.

As I held him, caressing that little face and checking out that little body, a battle of feelings began to overwhelm me.

How can I reasonably give this child a stable home life when I am nowhere near knowing what I am going to do with my life next week, much less next year or five years from now? And to add a little life to that confusion doesn't seem fair . . . to either of us.

But on the other hand, this little one is so much a part of me. Just by touch I know he is mine, even though he doesn't look a bit like me.

He really didn't. He looked like a little fuzzball. His hair was so pale it could hardly be seen, and it was so sparse and fuzzy you would have thought you were touching an oversized peach, not a baby's head.

I wanted to take him home and cuddle him forever. At the same time, I secretly hoped someone would come cuddle me. I talked to him softly, letting my hair fall down in front and almost touch the baby. "God, what am I going to do? What do you want me to do?" For once I really wanted his answer.

After a while, the tormenting confusion left, and I knew the best answer. At least for that day. Roberta had spoken of foster care. A foster family could take care of the baby until I made my final decision. That way I wouldn't have to make a lifetime decision right away.

I buzzed the nurse. She sweetly took the baby, then returned with release papers. The papers said the adoption agency could take the baby from the hospital and place it in foster care for a few days.

Jan appeared about ten-fifteen. "I just saw him, Julie. He's beautiful. I hate to say this, but he is far prettier than Stevie was."

"Thanks," I said softly.

"Here, open this." Jan handed me a package wrapped in paper decorated with rainbows.

I hesitated. *Please,* I thought, *no more socks.* I opened it slowly. A smile caught my mouth, and my heart warmed. I lifted out a beautiful pink silky-type nightgown and robe to match. "Oh, Jan."

She just smiled, her green eyes twinkling.

"Thank you so much." I leaned over and gave her one of my rare hugs.

"What are you going to do, Julie?"

"Oh, Jan." I began to cry. "I don't know. I just don't know."

17

MY bowl of Crisp Crunchies were no longer crisp, nor did they crunch. Soggy lumps, like swollen maggots, were lying there. No longer did they dance with anticipation. They were dead.

Dumping the mess into the sink, I got a dry bowl and started over. I wanted to eat before Stephanie arrived.

Perhaps this time no one would call attempting to gossip with my mother about the subject of the year: me. Most people didn't know Mom went back to work yesterday. So they continued calling to discuss my situation with her.

I could feel their embarrassment trickle through the phone as they attempted to cover their awkwardness about speaking with me. They talked nervously about inane things like the weather or their dog. You would think I'd never had a baby.

When I came home from the hospital, I unrealistically expected things to have changed. I don't know what I expected to be different. The furniture was unmoved. We sat at the same places to eat dinner. My room was just as I had left it, except the bed had clean sheets. My diary still lay open where I had attempted to write about labor.

Everyone came and went at the same times. All was the same.

But all was different.

I'd grown up. Too fast, for sure. I wished I could have stayed irresponsible for my allotted time. But no such luck. I knew it was going to be hard to return to school in the fall. My experiences had left me feeling awkward and out of place among my friends. Their gossip and arguments didn't interest me anymore. But I was jealous of them, and of Matt and Tammy. They had retained their innocence.

Tammy was pouting every time I saw her. She would turn her head and walk the other direction. She was angry with me for not bringing the baby home. She wanted to hold him, baby-sit him, and change his diapers. She thought I'd deserted him.

I overheard Matt and Tammy talking about me the day I got home from the hospital. I was about to leave my room when I heard their voices muffled in the hall.

"It's a good thing," I heard Matt say. "I wouldn't want a screaming baby around while I try to study."

I didn't wait to hear Tammy's answer. I turned and flung myself onto the bed and sobbed into my pillow.

Tension as thick and tough as a cheap steak filled our house for the remainder of the week.

Dad certainly didn't know how to handle me. His conversation was limited to, "How are you feeling?" After asking that ten times, I think he decided I would always say, "Fine." Then the conversation would promptly stagnate, and he would revert to silence and look the other way.

Mom, on the other hand, chattered constantly. She tried to have something for me to do all the time. I never got a chance to think.

This week was going better. The family had stopped treating me like a fragile egg. Physically I was feeling better, too. The milk in my breasts was about dry, so they weren't full and heavy anymore and had stopped leaking. Too bad they couldn't stay that size. I'd have liked that a lot.

I couldn't get into my regular clothes yet. My stomach had lost all muscle tone. Extra skin rippled around me like Jell-O. I desperately hoped that would go away.

I finished my bowl of cereal as the doorbell rang.

Stephanie had ditched school to come see me. I had spoken to her last night for the first time since the baby was born. Before that, I could hardly talk to anyone without crying or falling asleep. Having a baby sure does weird things to your system.

I opened the door to see her eyes sparkle and dance with the excitement of seeing me. But her excitement turned to dismay when she saw my stomach. It still looked five months pregnant and must have shocked her.

"It'll go away," I assured her.

Relieved and rolling her eyes, she exclaimed, "Good." She bounced into the house, making herself at home on the sofa. "So," she said with a toss of her hair. "Tell me all about it."

I have never seen someone so intensely curious that they couldn't sit still. She bounced her crossed leg and rubbed her hands in anticipation.

"All about what?" I asked teasingly.

"All about the birth," she replied impatiently. "I want to know every little detail."

So I embarked on the journey, starting with the backaches. Whenever she sensed I had left something out, she probed until I returned an answer more suitable to her liking. We chatted like two little old ladies who had heard the latest gossip at the beauty shop.

When I finally finished my story, you would have thought someone we were talking about had entered the room. Our conversation stopped dead, and we suddenly had nothing more to say.

"I'd better go now," said Stephanie in her soft,

awkward voice. "Let me know when you feel up to a movie or something."

I figured she only offered out of courtesy. We said the polite good-byes of two strangers. I watched her walk to her bike, swing her leg over the seat, and take off in the direction of school. As I watched her pedal away, it reminded me again of the hot day when I met Kyle.

I hadn't seen him in over three months. It bothered me when I thought of how I treated him that day. I had held back all the patience and kindness God had just given me. I guess I hadn't realized I had enough to share.

It was weird to think Kyle didn't even know he was the father of a seven-and-a-half-pound boy. Kyle, a father. Just saying it sounded ridiculous. I could never truthfully picture Kyle as a father.

But he did have rights to the baby. The adoption agency had said they would call me as soon as they had contacted him regarding the adoption. I'd told them I wouldn't make my final decision until I knew whether Kyle would sign relinquishment papers.

It was so hard to wait.

18

THE phone rang steadily, over and over. It stopped before I thought to answer it. The song that had sent me rushing into the past had long since ended. I glanced at the clock. Two hours had passed.

I was glad I had been alone. It was good to cry and think without anybody barging in. With a heavy sigh, I finished folding the clothes for Mom and placed them on her bed.

The phone began to ring again. I took a deep breath and headed for my room. I sat on the bed and slowly picked up the receiver.

Roberta's voice sounded typically matter-of-fact. "We finally reached Kyle."

"Oh," I tried to say calmly as my heart jumped wildly in my chest.

Roberta's voice came again. "He signed the papers."

I was afraid to ask, yet I had to know. "Which ones?" My heart felt like a caged tiger, beating itself against the bars confining it.

Roberta paused. "The waiver."

I caught my breath. His choice to sign Denial of Paternity would have been less of a blow than this. To me, the waiver declared, "I don't care. I don't care about the baby, I don't care about Julie. I don't care."

The words of the waiver danced through my mind: I do hereby waive my right to further notice of adoption planning of said child. It is fully understood by me that with the signing of this document I give up any further rights to said child.

Roberta interrupted my thoughts. "Have you made your final decision?"

"Yes," I said with determination. My last hope of Kyle's love was gone with the dash of a pen. Oh, God, I felt my heart cry, please take care of my little boy. Aloud I said, "I love him, Roberta. But he needs a family."

I tried to listen to her instructions through a pain-clouded mind.

"We will meet at Wohlford's Family Restaurant in Santa Rosa. Ten o'clock tomorrow morning. OK?"

I stifled a sob. "Yes."

I hung up the phone heavily. I let the sobs overtake me. I'd tried to pretend the adoption didn't make me sad. I'd been angry at the world for allowing this to happen to girls like me. I'd been depressed enough to fill two hospital wards. I'd even felt no one loved me or cared about this.

Mostly, I'd come to realize all of my feelings were OK. It was OK to cry. It was OK to feel empty. And it was OK to feel peace that I'd done the right thing.

• • •

The sun hurt my eyes. I wore sunglasses to hide the red, swollen lids. I walked quickly, head down, to Jan's house.

Jan cried with me. Then we prayed. As always, I felt a new strength to face my world at home.

And I would need that strength more than ever. At dinner I would announce my decision.

19

I watched the clock by the side of my bed, carefully calculating each minute as it ticked by. Each minute winged my little boy farther from me and closer to his new parents.

I could picture them as they drove to the airport. They would get there far too early. Eager, so eager, they would pace the airport, hand in sweaty hand. They'd stop to buy a sweet roll and coffee and find they could not eat or drink.

They would stand by the tinted windows, watching each plane as it arrived. An eternity of minutes would pass until the plane pulled up to the arm that reaches out to gather the passengers into the terminal.

With hearts in their throats, they'd move silently to the roped-off area into which they are not allowed. They would wait. They would search the arms of every *woman passenger. They would search for the flash of lavender indicating Roberta had arrived.*

They would begin to lose hope as the stream of passengers dwindled to a trickle of stragglers. Their hands would clutch tightly as a woman approached. In her arms would be a bundle with only a fuzzy fair head peeking out of the soft blanket.

The woman would speak. "Are you Mrs. Booth?" Roberta would nod. "And you?" she asks formally.

The man, tall and fair-headed, would speak hesitantly, introducing himself and his wife to Roberta.

Smiling, Roberta would say coyly, "I think I have something that belongs to you."

With that, both would begin to cry. I could imagine how anxious the woman would be to touch this little one she had waited and prayed for, for so long.

Roberta would wisely instruct them to sit, and she would place my little boy into their eager arms. They'd coo and cry over him as if they had birthed him themselves.

They'd sign the remaining papers without pausing to read them and then change him into the blue outfit they had brought for him. Roberta would leave to catch her return plane.

The couple would sit for a while longer, unable to get up. They fear if they do, their dream might burst. But then the baby starts to cry, and they head to the car where they will feed him.

I could imagine the man driving more cautiously than he ever had before. He was taking the three of them home, to their home.

Oh, God. My heart wanted to break.

...

The minutes tick off portions of my life. Not one can ever be retrieved. Nothing about my past can be changed. The choices I've made will affect me forever.

My future will be different because I'm a different person than when I met Kyle. I'm not desperate for love and acceptance anymore. Sometimes I don't *feel* loved, yet I *know* I am. God loves me. And he promises that my present and my future are in his careful, loving hands.

Sometimes that promise is all I have to keep me going.

Other Living Books Best-sellers

400 CREATIVE WAYS TO SAY I LOVE YOU by Alice Chapin. Perhaps the flame of love has almost died in your marriage, or you have a good marriage that just needs a little spark. Here is a book of creative, practical ideas for the woman who wants to show the man in her life that she cares. 07-0919-5

ANSWERS by Josh McDowell and Don Stewart. In a question-and-answer format, the authors tackle sixty-five of the most-asked questions about the Bible, God, Jesus Christ, miracles, other religions, and Creation. 07-0021-X

BUILDING YOUR SELF-IMAGE by Josh McDowell and Don Stewart. Here are practical answers to help you overcome your fears, anxieties, and lack of self-confidence. Learn how God's higher image of who you are can take root in your heart and mind. 07-1395-8

COME BEFORE WINTER AND SHARE MY HOPE by Charles R. Swindoll. A collection of brief vignettes offering hope and the assurance that adversity and despair are temporary setbacks we can overcome! 07-0477-0

DR. DOBSON ANSWERS YOUR QUESTIONS by Dr. James Dobson. In this convenient reference book, re-nowned author Dr. James Dobson addresses heartfelt concerns on many topics, including questions on marital relationships, infant care, child discipline, home man-agement, and others. 07-0580-7

THE EFFECTIVE FATHER by Gordon MacDonald. A practi-cal study of effective fatherhood based on biblical principles. 07-0669-2

FOR MEN ONLY edited by J. Allan Petersen. This book deals with topics of concern to every man: the business world, marriage, fathering, spiritual goals, and problems of living as a Christian in a secular world. 07-0892-X

FOR WOMEN ONLY by Evelyn R. and J. Allan Petersen. This balanced, entertaining, and diversified treatment covers all the aspects of womanhood. 07-0897-0

GIVERS, TAKERS, AND OTHER KINDS OF LOVERS by Josh McDowell and Paul Lewis. Bypassing generalities about love and sex, this book answers the basics: What-ever happened to sexual freedom? Do men respond differ-ently than women? Here are straight answers about God's plan for love and sexuality. 07-1031-2

Other Living Books Best-sellers

HINDS' FEET ON HIGH PLACES by Hannah Hurnard. A classic allegory of a journey toward faith that has sold more than a million copies! 07-1429-6 *Also on Tyndale Living Audio 15-7426-4*

HOW TO BE HAPPY THOUGH MARRIED by Tim LaHaye. A valuable resource that tells how to develop physical, mental, and spiritual harmony in marriage. 07-1499-7

JOHN, SON OF THUNDER by Ellen Gunderson Traylor. In this saga of adventure, romance, and discovery, travel with John—the disciple whom Jesus loved—down desert paths, through the courts of the Holy City, and to the foot of the cross as he leaves his luxury as a privileged son of Israel for the bitter hardship of his exile on Patmos. 07-1903-4

LET ME BE A WOMAN by Elisabeth Elliot. This best-selling author shares her observations and experiences of male-female relationships in a collection of insightful essays. 07-2162-4

LIFE IS TREMENDOUS! by Charlie "Tremendous" Jones. Believing that enthusiasm makes the difference, Jones shows how anyone can be happy, involved, relevant, productive, healthy, and secure in the midst of a high-pressure, commercialized society. 07-2184-5

MORE THAN A CARPENTER by Josh McDowell. A hard-hitting book for people who are skeptical about Jesus' deity, his resurrection, and his claim on their lives. 07-4552-3 *Also on Tyndale Living Audio 15-7427-2*

QUICK TO LISTEN, SLOW TO SPEAK by Robert E. Fisher. Families are shown how to express love to one another by developing better listening skills, finding ways to disagree without arguing, and using constructive criticism. 07-5111-6

REASONS by Josh McDowell and Don Stewart. In a convenient question-and-answer format, the authors address many of the commonly asked questions about the Bible and evolution. 07-5287-2

THE SECRET OF LOVING by Josh McDowell. McDowell explores the values and qualities that will help both the single and married reader to be the right person for someone else. He offers a fresh perspective for evaluating and improving the reader's love life. 07-5845-5

Other Living Books Best-sellers

THE STORY FROM THE BOOK. From Adam to Armageddon, this book captures the full sweep of the Bible's content in abridged, chronological form. Based on *The Book,* the best-selling, popular edition of *The Living Bible.* 07-6677-6

STRIKE THE ORIGINAL MATCH by Charles Swindoll. Swindoll draws on the best marriage survival guide–the Bible–and his 35 years of marriage to show couples how to survive, flex, grow, forgive, and keep romance alive in their marriage. 07-6445-5

THE STRONG-WILLED CHILD by Dr. James Dobson. Through these practical solutions and humorous anecdotes, parents will learn to discipline an assertive child without breaking his spirit and to overcome feelings of defeat or frustration. 07-5924-9 *Also on Tyndale Living Audio 15-7431-0*

SUCCESS! THE GLENN BLAND METHOD by Glenn Bland. The author shows how to set goals and make plans that really work. His ingredients of success include spiritual, financial, educational, and recreational balances. 07-6689-X

THROUGH GATES OF SPLENDOR by Elisabeth Elliot. This unforgettable story of five men who braved the Auca Indians has become one of the most famous missionary books of all time. 07-7151-6

TRANSFORMED TEMPERAMENTS by Tim LaHaye. An analysis of Abraham, Moses, Peter, and Paul, whose strengths and weaknesses were made effective when transformed by God. 07-7304-7

WHAT WIVES WISH THEIR HUSBANDS KNEW ABOUT WOMEN by Dr. James Dobson. A best-selling author brings us this vital book that speaks to the unique emotional needs and aspirations of today's woman. An immensely practical, interesting guide. 07-7896-0

WHAT'S IN A NAME? Linda Francis, John Hartzel, and Al Palmquist, Editors. This fascinating name dictionary features the literal meaning of hundreds of first names, character qualities implied by the names, and an applicable Scripture verse for each name. 07-7935-5

WHY YOU ACT THE WAY YOU DO by Tim LaHaye. Discover how your temperament affects your work, emotions, spiritual life, and relationships, and learn how to make improvements. 07-8212-7